Kingdom of Abel

-A Journey Not Their Own -

Gume Laurel III

CHAPTERS

Preface

An eruption of roaring fire clenched onto the growing smog over the battlefield, pulling itself higher into the sky as it emitted a foul black smoke too thick to see through, while the opposing armies of the foreign lands began their final wave of attacks.

The armies unknown to this once peaceful land, dressed in charcoal armor of metal, laced with rust and dents, raced into the dissipating battle, trampling over the charred dirt where there was once a lush forest that hid many secrets. The cries of warriors, both good and evil, accompanied by the clanking of sword striking sword, sounded out into the atmosphere as the war that was drawing to a close etched itself into history for future generations to recall and mourn over.

Dressed in long rugged robes of dark green wool, the king of this land stood, watching as the soil gifted to his dynasty was stained in dismay and death. He was standing in the eastern corner of the battlefield, where his army had established their territory, though the entire land was this king's by birthright.

Sweat built up in his closed fist, gripping tighter to the long golden staff he held, as his short and full dark brown beard, tainted by the smoke of flames, gently swayed in the wind. His beard was lightly highlighted with white hairs that proclaimed of his wisdom with age, and the indentations on his face, wrinkles sketched over time, had collected dirt and ash that began to silently clear as tears streamed down his face. The enemy had come into his land, and taken what was his.

"Enough," the king uttered beneath his breath, his words unheard due to the great volume of war ragging before him, even by his two personal guards that stood beside him, one two feet to his right, the other two feet to his left.

He took one step, and then another, toward the battle. As he continued to walk, his guards, without need of orders, immediately followed after him, unmoved from the waist up, their swords in their sheaths aside their left thighs, their shields in their left hand. Before the king took his seventh step, his guards, which were once at his sides, now positioned themselves two feet in front of, and two feet behind, their king. When the king took his ninth step, the guards pulled out their sharpened silver swords, and a high pitched ringing could be heard as their swords left their left sides, the blades rubbing against the hollowed interior of their sheaths.

With every step the king took, he drew closer to the battle zone. His long solid robes trailed inches behind him across the ground, gathering dirt and ash, while his golden crown that resembled a blossoming olive branch, bound into a circle, rested upon his head. Each blossom on his crown was carved from a single opal stone.

Thirteen steps, and the king was seven steps away from where the battle raged, where at that moment a warrior of the opposing side had caught eye of the traveling king. Thoughts of glory shot through this evil warrior's mind at the idea of being the one to slay the king of this land; the King of the East.

Upon the silver armored chests of the king's guards were carved olive trees that had many leaves, but bore no blossoms. Though this battle had gone for days, the swords of these guards had remained dry because they had been positioned aside their king day and night to protect him from any incoming dangers.

Fifteen steps, and the warrior of evil, who had his eyes fixed on the king, fully turned his entire body to face the king. He had become so engulfed with thoughts of grandeur for what he would be rewarded for taking down this king, that he had not taken notice of the guard that was approaching only three steps from him.

Sitting on the top of the king's golden staff was an olive blossom in bloom, shaped from pure stones of opal. Opal was a precious stone that was not common in this land, but instead a fine treasure that very few in the entire history of the eastern kingdom had ever come across because there was far more to this stone than mere beauty.

Sixteen steps, and the evil warrior raised his sword into the air, pride foaming over in his heart, and with the king's seventeenth step, the sword of his guard two steps ahead of him slayed the evil warrior who had been blinded to the guard by his own greed. The hearts of these evil warriors were so vile that even common sense and reasoning had no place in their minds.

Seventeen steps, and the guard two feet behind the king turned his back to the king's back, his eyes darting about, keeping close watch on surrounding and coming threats to the king.

As more steps were taken, more nearby enemy warriors began to make their way toward the king. If any came to attack from the king's front or left side, his guard before him quickly fought back for his king, and if a threat came from the king's back or right side, his guard behind him did the same just as quickly and fiercely.

By one hundred steps, the guards had taken down ten enemies each. At two hundred fifty steps, an additional thirty each had been stopped, and by the five hundredth step, the total for each guard was twice as much.

West of the battlefield, in the corner opposite to the king's camp, was the campsite of the evil forces the king and his men had been fighting against. The queen of this invading nation sat upon her small mobile throne of onyx, watching as the king strode toward her direction. Her elegantly thin black dress poured onto the ground, and her straight, shoulder length, ash colored hair blew carelessly in the soft, yet comfortless, wind. Two feet to her left, and two feet to her right, stood strong guards that protected her through the battle, both in heavy black armor that had not been damaged because they had not left their positions through the entire attack. On their plated chests were similar carvings to the ones the king's guards had, only the trees were dead and leafless.

By the five hundred twenty-fifth step, the king and his uninjured guards reached the clearing between the battle and the queen on her throne. The campsite was empty because the queen had sent every last warrior to fight, except for her two guards.

Twenty more steps and the king finally arrived before the queen, at which she rose from her seat, and stood before him as his guards returned to his right and left sides. The guards to her left and right drew their swords, seeing that the swords the king's guards wielded were no longer dry.

"You have taken what you came for," the king bellowed in his aging voice to the queen. "Why must you continue this destruction? Your war is not against this land."

"My war is against its people," she declared to the king, her crown, a circular silver carving of a leafless olive branch sitting atop her head.

"Then it is also with me," he replied to her, quickly losing his patience with the young queen, as was unusual for his dealings with her.

"I have claimed the lives of those I came to destroy, and in doing so have ensured that the western crown will stay upon my head," she explained to the king as her blood red lips bounced with every word unfolding from her mouth, her pale white cheeks only magnified by this. "The days will soon return when there will only be one crown to rule over both east and west. But until I see that day, and the single crown rests upon my head, know my heart's desire. It is to see the downfall of the Kingdom of Abel, and I will not exhaust my efforts until your kingdom in the east falls, whether you stand to defy me, or not, father."

"I only extended this battle so that you would leave, and more lives would be spared," the king said turning his back to his daughter, now looking to the great battle. "But I will do this no longer."

The king raised his staff into the air, and what seemed like a blast of a horn sounded out from the blossom that sat atop the end of his staff, echoing onto the battlefield, only meeting the ears of those who were in the army that fought for righteousness: those from the Kingdom of Abel, the kingdom of the east, the natives of this land. The king's army all began to retreat to their campsite east of the battlefield, while the army of the queen stood perplexed.

"Stop him!" the queen ordered the guard to her left.

The guard to her left charged at the king, and the guard to the king's right immediately met him, and they began to battle with their swords. These four guards were the swiftest, strongest, and most skilled of all the warriors in both kingdoms.

A sound like crashing waves on rocks came from the battlefield as the army of the queen celebrated at what they thought was the forfeit of the king's army, as the king's staff remained risen in the air.

"Don't let him lower his arms!" the queen screamed to the guard on her right, causing this guard to bolt toward the king, being thrust into a brawl with the king's other guard who had been waiting to fight.

The four guards fought fiercely; this was a perfectly even match.

Without warning, the king struck down his staff like an axe into the earth, the end with the blossom burying into the ground. The moment his staff met the dirt, patterns of what looked like lightning strands shot across the ground, from the point of the kings staff, to the battlefield; it was the earth cracking and splitting open. The evil army continued to cheer for what they thought was their victory, and without noticing, the earth beneath them began to shatter into pieces, breaking apart beneath them.

Wails were lifted into the sky from the evil forces as they fell into the earth that opened beneath their feet, consuming all of them. Watching helplessly, the queen began to grind her teeth, the opal blossom still planted in the ground, with the four guards continuing their endless fighting.

"What have you done?!" the queen screamed, stomping towards the king whose back was still turned to her. "Will you really bury them alive in the graves of our fathers before us?"

At this, a force shot from the buried blossom of precious stone into the ground behind the king, causing the queen to stop in her tracks, and even take steps back. The ground split open between the queen and the king, with the fighting guards left on the side of the king.

"Return to my side!" the queen commanded her guards, with them immediately returning, leaping over the three foot gap that the king had created. Though it was not wide, it went deep, and what was at the bottom of this pit was a horror too terrible for chance. "We must leave before this madman's power takes the best of him and we are banished to where all fear to tread."

The three raced away to the back end of the camp where the queen's carriage had been left, but there were no horses to be seen. Instead, her guards escorted her into her carriage, opening the door before her and shutting it behind her, and then went to the front of the carriage, kneeling down on their hands and knees, sticking their heads through the yokes that were used to attach to horses' necks to pull the carriage. With their breaths growing deeper and deeper, they began to take on the shape of horses. Their chests began to stretch out, with every breath being taken their chest inflating more and more, as their arms and legs became thick, their hands clenching into tight fists that then turned into hooves. The helmets covering their heads stretched down across the spines on their backs, turning into long coal colored manes, and their metal armor became a thick black coat of hair, covering the whole of their bodies. The bottom of their jaws dropped into long snouts, and flaring nostrils at the ends spouted out steam so focused it could set water to boil. They stood taller than any normal stallion, and had far greater strength and speed.

The two guards, now massive black stallions, cried out dominant neighs, pounded at the ground with their heavy hooves, and raced away toward the west, pulling the queen in her carriage, which bounced violently behind them as they sped away.

The gap in the ground that had formed between the king and queen then reached to where her vacant onyx throne remained, and the earth devoured her throne. This small plot of ground then sealed itself shut again, in a fraction of the time it had taken to first open.

Section by section, the ground across the battlefield began to become whole once again and roughly returned to the way it originally was before opening. Fragments of smoke rolled over the now calm battlefield as dust and dirt lifted off the ground and into the wind. While this all occurred, the eyes of the king had not left the battlefield. Where there was once a great forest, now only emptiness could be found. There was now a void in the land that would take generations to refill, leaving the king with only memories of its former beauty.

Gently, the king lifted his royal staff from the ground. There was a still and eerie silence that had fallen over the land. The eastern army did not shout or celebrate because they took no satisfaction in the loss of their fallen brothers from the west. What was only passing seconds, instead felt like hours. The roaring silence was only broken by the soft whisper of the breeze declaring a victory for the eastern army. Seconds turned into minutes as the king continued to take in the view of his destroyed lands.

Without saying a word, the king began to walk back toward his army's campsite with both his guards loyally keeping their positions to his right and left as they marched across the abandoned field. There were no bodies, and there were no weapons; only gritty churned soil to be seen across this field. As he quietly walked back to the east, he looked up to the sky to see a white eagle gliding majestically on the winds above the smoke and stench of death that hovered in the air. It was flying east, toward his kingdom, which was two days travel on foot from this war site.

"Did she hear of him?" the queen of the eastern lands questioned her king as he walked into their bedroom, quickly shutting the doors behind him, while she sat next to a baby carriage drowning in white silk sheets, protected by a long white netted veil that hung from the ceiling high above their heads.

Very few candles were left burning this night, and no other eyes had been given permission to look at what these two gazed upon. The queen's question was the first voice to break the silence that had taken place for the past couple days in this room. Even the newborn had refrained from crying, as though he knew to keep himself secret.

"No," he responded, walking behind her, putting his right hand on her right shoulder as both of them peered through the veil, into the carriage that held a baby that was days old, his porcelain skin revealing his veins. "She knows nothing of him. It is to her understanding that all of his kind has been destroyed. The east is safe, again... for now."

A brief pause came as their tired eyes observed his tiny sleeping body.

"So much destruction," the old queen whispered looking to the soft red cheeks of the newborn, "over a baby."

Kingdom of Abel
- A Journey Not Their Own -

Elijah's Mourning

A peaceful mist hung over the Kingdom of Abel, the prosperous eastern kingdom, as the sun began to rise facing toward the backside of the castle, the streams of burning light striking into the warming sky, conquering over the shades of dark blue that had reigned in the darkness before dawn, gladly giving up their place on high for the new day. Throughout the streets an echo of silence became interrupted as the markets of the city began to open, and people quickly trickled into the roads for another day of life in this tranquil city. At the far east of the town was the magnificent castle of the royal family that governed the eastern realm of this land. Dew that took rest on the smooth white brick of the castle began to glisten in the light of the sun while keepers of the torches along the great wall that enclosed this city and castle began to extinguish the flames of the torches that bore continuous light through the nighttime. Absolute darkness had never fallen on the kingdom; there was always light, no matter how bright or dim.

Hidden beneath the leaves of tall green hedges that surrounded the castle walls were birds that sang songs that could only be heard this hour everyday, giving permission for the sun to rise and for the morning to blossom like a flower in spring. A great distance above the choir of birds was a wide balcony that led to the royal bedroom and, King Seth, the ruler of this land, was standing on it, leaning on the brick wall of the balcony that overlooked the city. His eyes looked past the city that had woken, to the immense forest that grew on the other side of the white stone wall that protected his kingdom. Past the long trail of woods was a great meadow that had grown in the past several years, which was hidden behind the tall trees that still stood in the forest. It was the land where the last war waged by his kingdom had taken place. Beyond the meadow, which from where the king stood was too far to see with natural eyes, was a great fog that was always too heavy to see past. Hidden behind the fog was the western land, which was under the ruling of the Kingdom of Cain. None from the east ever thought to go there, or even spoke of this land because it was a land of banished evils that were bathed in shadow. The sun could not shine there because the entire area was covered in a thick blanket of darkness that fell long ago, when a beast of legend had been released in the west.

There were many stories passed down from one generation to the next detailing the history of the lands in which these people lived.

At the earliest point in recorded history, there were seven tribes of people that were all grouped together, about one thousand people in all, not including children. There was no need for structured government because all the people lived in harmony with each other, none stealing, cheating, lying, or wronging each other in any way, or wronging the One who had placed them there in this land. The One was a voice that called from the heavens, who no man had ever seen. He dwelled high beyond the reach of the furthest stars, but when the One spoke, appeared to be all around. A great storm cloud would cover over the people, and the voice would then speak, as though dwelling within an inner light encased in the storm. His voice was like crashing thunder rolling over the earth, causing those in the One's presence to fall as though dead, struck with fear at this matchless power. He had created the land, and all within it, along with the people, and all that was in them.

These thousand people were camped in tents that were in the east, though they never left to any other area to even know they were in the east, in a wide clearing that was surrounded by forests and rivers. One morning, the voice from the sky bellowed down to the people, calling forth one particular man from each of the seven tribes. In great fear and reverence, the men came out from their tents, and the voice instructed them to walk further east within the great clearing. After ten steps, the voice ordered for four of the men to stop walking, and stand still. The other three took another forty steps, and were all told to stop in their tracks as well. At each of their feet was an olive tree branch that had been bound into a circle. Each branch was decorated in brilliant green leaves, and had closed flower buds that had not yet blossomed.

The three men were told to pick up the circular branch that was at their feet, and place it on their heads. The three did as they were told, and upon the head of one of the three the buds began to blossom, revealing the most beautiful pedals of white that had never been seen before this day, but on the heads of the other two, the buds stayed shut. The One then told the two with blossomless branches to take off the branches from their heads, and to bury the circular branches in the ground because there would only be one crown upon one head to govern the people in the east. The two men did this, immediately burying the branches at the spots they had first picked them up. The man with the blossoming branch upon his head was then told by the voice to take another seventy steps forward, and then stand still.

The roaring voice then gave instructions to the seven men.

To the four men who stood ten steps away from where they first started, the One gave them dimensions for monumental walls that they and their tribes were to build. These walls would protect the seven camp tribes, closing them in, but the walls would be so large that they would exceed the current size of the thousand-member camp. It would be seventy times the size currently needed, which was miles long all around, in the shape of a square, nearly running along the edge of the surrounding forests.

To the two men who buried the olive branches at their feet, the voice gave them dimensions for a castle they and their two tribes were to build that would house the ruler of all the tribes. It would be grand, ascending high into the clouds, and unlike any structure that had ever been seen before, or even imagined.

As for the man with the olive branch upon his head, the voice within the storm clouds declared him king over all the people of the seven tribes. Where he stood now, he was to place his throne from where he would reign. The branch would be his crown, and once the building of the walls and castle were complete, a replica of the crown was to be made of gold and opal to replace this current crown. He was to bury the branch that blossomed on his head behind the castle, outside of the kingdom walls, in a part of the forest that the people had never ventured into that was a couple days worth of walking away. The king was told to make this journey alone.

To the tribe of this new king, they were given orders to aid in the building of the wall and castle by getting materials the One divinely provided by placing them in the surrounding forests, and by construction of the kingdom. The king was to oversee all the work, and make sure it was all done as the voice had instructed. Along with instructions, the voice told these seven men that what they were building, this grand kingdom, was for a king the One would send to them at a later time, so this caused the men to increase in the perfection of skill with which they made the walls and castle.

Many years went by until the kingdom in the east was completed, but once it had been done, no eye had yet seen anything like this in the land. The first six tribes were ordered from then on to live within the walls of the kingdom, and to establish a city that the king would rule over. The seventh tribe of the pronounced king was ordered to live within the castle, and be direct servants to the king.

Before, these tribes had lived in tents made of cloth and branches, but now, they would live in a city of stone.

From then on, the seven tribes became one people, and there was no division between them. They lived in peace under the ruling of the king. None argued against his place of authority because the One had sovereignly placed him there, and all the people were witness to this from the day this one man was called out of the seven.

The One then sent from the sky a cloud that settled atop a flattened section of the castle's roof, and when the cloud dispersed, it left behind a sacred garden in which only the king could enter. The garden was encased by tall and thin white marble walls, in the shape of an octagon, with a deeply rooted olive tree growing in the center of the garden, its roots growing within the walls of the castle, which had thick branches spread out high as a covering to the garden, sealing the room shut. From the lower branches were bloomed flowers that had precious stones of opal within them that would release a white light which would reflect onto the surface of a small pond that was beside the olive tree, creating a dimly lit garden of white from the flowers, and dark blue hues from the pond. There was a double door entrance, formed from silver, which was a foot less tall than the wall, and just less than three feet wide. Within the walls of the garden, the One then spoke to the king, giving him orders and regulations for the people. The One now only spoke to the king, coming as a cool breeze into the garden made for fellowship between the king and the One. As the king spent time in the presence of the voice, he was drawn close to the One, and this king found a special place in the heart of the One. The voice would share secrets with the king, and gave him insight to the land that, much of the time, was only for the king to know, and not the people of the kingdom.

The voice shared with the king of the times before men walked the earth, when the One carved the mountains of the land with his breath, and called up from the ground seeds to sprout into the lush forests that now surrounded the kingdom. He told the king about creating the smallest of animals, and the largest of beasts that roamed the land, flew in the sky, swam in the waters, and burrowed in the ground. Most of these animals the voice spoke of had never been seen by the eyes of anyone from the newly formed kingdom because they had always lived in the clearing, which was now a developing city within the walls. The king alone had seen some of these animals when he traveled out to bury the first crown, and recorded what he saw in a journal he kept hidden in this royal garden.

The One told the king of His armies that stood before Him, where He sat on a throne, surrounded by endless light, in a place too far for any man to walk to in this life. The voice spoke of a great being that once stood as a prince before Him, but this being's heart had become wicked, its desires grown dark, lusting after the power and authority that its creator held. This prince also convinced a great number of the One's army that he should rule over them, bring shadow to the One's courts. Because there was no shifting shadow in the presence of the One, He cast away this being, and its followers, from His presence, downward to the depths far beneath the sky, to the earth. The voice then came down as a violent storm to this land, where the beings of deceit had fallen to, prepared to pronounce judgments over these rebels. The lead of these rebels had taken on the form of a grotesque dragon, and its followers had morphed into the forms of snakes, scorpions, lizards, spiders, and various venomous creatures that crawled along the ground, though they were giant in size.

At the sound of the thundering voice, the army of rebels, and the dragon, all fled in fear, to the deepest depths of the oceans, trying to hide from the authority of the One who had thrown them down. The voice called the rebels back up from the ocean, including the dragon. The rebel army was then struck down even further than the earth, to deep caves beneath the surface of the land, through two entrances in the land. One was in the east, at the bottom of a massive lake, and the other was in the west, at the bottom of a great pit that lay surrounded by jagged mountains. The voice then sealed these entrances with onyx stones that could only be removed by a royal bloodline the voice would call forth at a later time. As for the dragon, the leader of this riot, the voice banished it back to the depths of the oceans, at the deepest point, in volcanic pits that boiled over with burning saltwater. Chains of onyx were formed to bind this dragon, and he was to be left there. These rebels were never seen again by any other creation.

The voice told the king of this tale because the royal bloodline that could open these entranceways would begin with him alone, to then be passed on through the future generations that came from him. From the time of the first king, this bloodline was maintained by the kings' children being forbidden to have children of their own unless the kings' child was crowned. The kings and their offspring were to be on guard with this precious gift because once set free, these beasts could not easily be stopped. The only way one of these beasts could be slain by the hands of man was if a member of the royal bloodline obtained a six-piece suit that the voice had forged, and placed on the earth; each of the six pieces hidden in separate locations across the earth, in places that would take months, even years, to reach from the eastern kingdom. This special warrior suit would give its wearer the same strength as the thundering voice Himself, but would reject anyone who was not a direct member of the royal bloodline who wore it, causing them to die.

Time went on, and as this first king grew old, he prepared one of his sons that the One chose to become the next king, training him in leadership, and guiding him in fellowship with the One. When a certain day came, the voice whispered to the king that it was time to pass the crown on to his son, and for the king to then enter the sacred garden for the final time. A great ceremony was held to usher in the new king, and at the end of it, the first king entered into the garden, and was never seen again. When his son, the new king, went into the sacred garden, the body of his father was nowhere to be found. Though no trace of the previous king was ever found, the voice told the newly crowned king he had taken his father away to stand before the throne of the One, beyond the furthest reaches of the sky.

This pattern continued for many generations, and the kingdom grew numerically within the towering walls that the first generation had built, living in peace, as there seemed to be no other people in all the earth, but the voice from the sky never grew as close to any other king as He had with the first one.

The thundering voice then decided to no longer come down to the earth, except to only briefly meet with the eastern kings in the sacred garden when it was needed. The rules and laws given to the first king were to be passed down through the kings over the generations. Because of this, before the end of the fifth king's reign, the voice that thundered from the sky sent to him four guardians that stood before the voice's throne beyond the stars. These four, having the continuous appearance of men, had the ability to take on the form of different animals, but always bore the color white, whether it be as skin, fur, feather, or scale. They were bound to the royal bloodline, and were to defend them at all costs. Unless there was a time of war, or risk of danger for the king, they were never to be seen. For most of their time on earth, they were left to dwell in the sacred garden. These four were known as the Diadem.

During the reign of the seventh king, four of the king's five sons ventured into the forested area outside the kingdom walls, in the western direction. After about two days of exploring on foot, they came across a part of the forest that was filled with trees that went higher than any other trees known to these people. From their branches hung bundles of assorted fruits that were much larger than normal, a single bundle enough to feed off of for a week once they were harvested. Exotic birds of fantastic warm colors and spotted designs nested in these fruit filled trees, and sang songs in ways never heard before. Upon returning to the kingdom with word of this new land, the four sons asked to be released from the kingdom to begin a settlement in this special part of the forest. At their request, the king gave them permission, with the ultimatum that they would have to lose their birthrights, titles as princes, and their royal privileges would be revoked, so that this new settlement would remain under the ruling of the kingdom, and any potential for an uprising would be prevented.

Only one of the sons agreed to this. His birthrights, title, and privileges were taken from him, and he was sent out with forty people from the kingdom's city. In the forest, they began a small village beneath the shade of the great fruit trees, and daily were in awe at the unique wildlife and plants that revealed themselves to these people from the eastern kingdom. Though away from the kingdom, they found peace. If there were to be announcements or news from the kingdom, the king would send to this village a messenger to keep them informed. The villagers never left the shade of the forest, and found everything they needed in their area.

A soft knocking came from the massive marble entrance door of the room the king was watching from. He turned his head sideways, to the left, while the door slowly opened, creaking as it did.

"Elijah is waiting for you," the old and soft voice of his wife spoke as she stood in the open doorway as she held tightly onto the iron doorknob, supporting herself because she had grown tired in her old age. "Why are you late this morning? It is not like you to be late, especially with the trip you depart for today."

"Time has gotten the best of me this morning, Mary," Seth said as he turned his whole body toward her direction.

Their wrinkled faces told stories of past trials they had gone through in the keeping of peace for this land. He slowly paced to the door, reaching for his golden staff that was now used more for a walking cane than it was to show his authority, yet the opal blossom at the top end of the staff still glistened as brilliantly as it had the day it was first formed.

"Time has gotten the best of both of us," Mary said as Seth took hold of his staff, and supported his old body with it. "I don't know why we both haven't left this life yet."

"Our time has not yet come to its end," he told her as she took hold of his open left arm to support her as they both walked out of the room and into the wide hallway, where the five maidens that would tend to the queen were waiting for her. "We still have things to complete here in this land. Our end is close. I will not doubt that because our age only has that to say. But for now, joy shall be our strength while we wait for our journey's end."

"Elijah." Seth called out as he walked into an outdoor garden that lay behind the castle, surrounded by tall walls of white marble that reached two stories high, keeping it private for the royal family.

"Here I am," a young voice answered back as Seth walked into the middle of the garden where a small grey stone fountain of water that had designs of angelic beings carved into it rested, while the trickling of the splashing fountain water removed the silence between their exchanging of words.

From behind a wall of bushes came a young man dressed in a rugged dark brown tunic, with skin the color of sand not yet soaked by the sea. Untamed wavy black hair grew from his head, shimmering a dark aqua color whenever the sun struck it with beams of light. His thin body walked toward the fountain, coming from the direction Seth was looking to, his glistening sea-blue eyes looking to his father.

"Forgive my being late," Seth said taking a step forward, his long dark green robes dragging along the ground, collecting bits of grass and fallen leaves as it did. "I lost track of time, and it was late into the morning before I found it again."

"There is no need to apologize, my king," Elijah replied to him as he reached the fountain, and stood feet away from Seth. "Did the queen find you? After you didn't come, she set out in search of you."

"Yes," the tired voice of the king bellowed, his brown eyes peering from behind his large cheeks. "She found me. If she hadn't, I would have been much later, but enough of that. We will leave for the meadow within the next few moments. Our travel guards should be prepared with a carriage outside these walls surrounding this garden by now. Get your things, and we will depart."

Seth and Mary loved Elijah dearly, and took care of him as their fourth child, though he was not their son by blood. Since Elijah had reached the age of seven, he became an apprentice to Seth, learning all there was to know about the land, and how to govern it best. Elijah would learn from Seth for the first six days of every week, and on the seventh, rest, so to prepare for the next six days. Seth had taught him to fight with many different weapons used in battles, filled him with knowledge of their land, understanding that was rare to find, wisdom in leading others, and the ways of the voice that once spoke from the sky. With these five things, Elijah would be able to take the throne in confidence when the day was to come.

"Why does the mist grow so heavy there?" Seth quizzed his son, pointing to the great fog in the distant, yet visible, westward view, as they stood in the great meadow where there was once a forest.

The carriage they had ridden out to this place on, along with the guards who came to keep watch over the king and prince, were left at the edge of the remaining forest area.

"The curse placed on the land there," Elijah answered. "Darkness fell over the west after they released a beast from beneath the earth. The fog bounds that darkness to the west."

"Would that be reason enough?" Seth questioned again as the gentle wind grazed through the tall and thin grass of the meadow that they stood in.

"I suppose." Elijah said, questioning himself in his head.

"Very well, then," the king told him as he looked back to his son. "But remember, things do not just happen, nor are things a certain way for a single reason. Every one thing is the way it is because of a series of things preceding it. If we do not know something's beginning, we will surely never know its end."

Elijah looked to the ground to see the lush bounty of grass growing all around him, swaying back and forth to the melody of the wind streaming about the meadow.

"This is the land," Elijah began to say in a way that caused Seth to turn away from his son. "The land that was once the home of my people."

"We both know this." Seth told him, a sour taste of mourning on his tongue. "What causes you to say it?"

"Because I can hear their cries," Elijah said, kneeling on his right knee, putting his hands that both had brown rough leather wrapped around his palms, like gloves, against the earth. "They cry of their innocence. They weren't guilty, nor in need of punishment."

"Many aren't that find misfortune." Seth comforted as he walked to Elijah, and put his wrinkled hand on his son's boney shoulder. "And their voices fell silent years ago, Elijah. What you hear is your own soul's wounds from that day. But now is not the time to remember a past that is not pleasant. There will be wars in the future that will remind us of past horrors, but now is a time for peace."

Elijah stood, and looked to his father, with his endless blue eyes swelling, about to burst and release rivers of tears that were the evidence of the pain he had yet to let go, which paved a way for fear to burrow in his heart.

"We must move on with today's lessons." Seth said to Elijah, avoiding further discussion on the past of this area, attempting to clog his emotions from flowing. "It will be nightfall soon."

"They've past the fog barrier!" a thin man with porcelain colored skin yelled running into the center of the village where many of the people had gathered in a panic. "They will be here shortly!"

"That gives us no time to prepare!" a woman carrying a baby wrapped in large leaves yelled as others began to chaotically run, spreading the warning that this messenger had brought them.

Above her, past the lowest branches of the trees that covered this village, flocks of beautifully colored birds terrifyingly flew away from their nests above the village, their loose feathers falling from their darting bodies, and to the ground where the crowds stomped about. From their beaks came sounds of fear that the people had never heard before.

"Enough!" an elder of these people shouted, causing complete silence to fall over the people surrounding him, as he walked to the center of the village, dressed in light colored moss, with long and frizzy faded orange hair that had weeds entangled into it swaying as an echo to his steps. "The western armies will be arriving much sooner than we anticipated. We must evacuate this place at once, and leave for the Kingdom of Abel. King Seth will give us protection there, behind the walls where our forefathers first came from!"

Just as he finished his announcement, a low rumbling noise developed, coming from the west. Stomping of a running warriors lifted into the forest, and the battle cries of this great army broke the hearts of the villagers. Bright lights began to shoot forth from the western side of the forest, followed by the sounds of trees that reached high into the heavens crashing to earth, their barks shattering like glass as they hit the ground.

"They're almost here!" a voice shouted as the village once again became filled with a chaos that had no end, and the people frantically grabbed what belongings they could carry, running east, in the direction of the Kingdom of Abel.

A tall and pale young man with an unshaved face suddenly ran past the elder who was scurrying away, sprinting toward a small hut made of material supplied by the forest. The young man pushed open the purple sheets that hung as a door, and entered the small hut made of branches and moss, to find his wife sitting on the ground, holding a baby wrapped in dark purple sheets, just like the ones for the door, tightly against her chest.

"They've reached the forest," he told her as he knelt before his wife, putting his large hand over the head of the baby that had been born just days before. "There is no time to stay still."

"What can we do?" she asked hopelessly as tears began to roll from her midnight blue eyes, and down her nearly transparent cheek, her skin pale due to living in the shade of the forest. "We cannot outrun the western military. They are too many, and so close."

The sounds of horses pounding against the earth suddenly shook the tiny hut and ground, the vibrations striking against the racing pulses of these two parents.

"The eastern armies have arrived!" the man said, jumping up, and opening the curtain door for the woman to see warriors dressed in silver armor upon white horses racing by their hut.

"We are still not safe," she said in despair.

"Do not give up yet," he commanded her, turning back towards her to help her get to her feet, as she continued to hold tightly onto their son.

"Women and children onto the carriages!" one of the leaders of the army of the east ordered in a shout, riding on his tall white horse. "Now!"

Holding tightly onto his wife, the man pulled her in the direction of one of the four large topless carriages made of wood that were being loaded with the women and children from the village.

"Hurry," he told her as they reached the carriage, and he helped her on, nearly having to force her into it, her short curly black hair bouncing at every move she made.

"And what of you?" she asked him as the crowd of women and children continued to pour onto the carriage, pushing her toward the middle of the carriage, away from her husband who could not join her.

"I will find you in the city!" he shouted to her, trying to allow his voice to reach her through the confusing cries and sounds of the approaching western army destroying the forest as they neared the village.

"What?!" she cried back to him, pushing her way to the side of the sturdy wagon, protecting her newborn from being pushed or harmed.

"I will find you in the city!" he exclaimed once more, rushing to the side of the carriage where she stood, as it suddenly began to be carried away by horses that were directed by riders from the army.

"Don't leave me!" she began crying as he walked alongside the carriage with her.

His fast paced walking turned into jogging, but within seconds he found himself running alongside the wagon, his wife not taking her eyes off of her husband, her sight only blurred by her tears.

"I must!" he yelled to her, losing breath as he ran as fast as he could, slowly falling behind the side of the wagon that was gaining speed. "I will find you in the city!"

The wife cried out to him as the carriage became too fast for him to keep up with at all, and he lost the strength to attempt to remain running beside it. Out of breath, he watched as the large carriage filled with women and children raced off into the distance.

"I fear the city I will meet you in will not be one in this lifetime," he whispered as he gasped to catch his breath, the battle cry of the opposing army intensifying as it drew closer.

With his arms wrapped around the sides of his cramping stomach, he turned back to face the west, and saw the great army of the Queen of the West enter into his village atop large black horses. They had come at a greater speed than imagined. He looked in horror as the Western warriors swung their weapons at the defenseless forest dwellers, without any sign of hope for their survival.

The wife cried, holding her son close to her, looking at his small face that resembled his father's. His feet nudged at her chest as she held him tightly, while his large red cheeks pushed up against his closed eyes. Amidst the darkness surrounding this mother and child, a hope could be heard with each weak beat of the baby's heart. In his mother's arms, his eyelids slowly stretched themselves open, exposing his watery eyes. A sudden concern filled the mother as she noticed a light reflecting off of her son's eyes that were looking straight up toward the trees.

An eerie emotion struck her as the violent carriage ride caused the group to be tossed about. She looked up to the sky that could barely be seen through all the tree branches, and saw burning flames above the branches.

"The queen has sent a flock of phoenix!" a child's voice cried from the other side of the carriage, the child pointing her finger up to the sky.

All the women and children began to scream as they looked up to see that they were being stalked by a flock of large birds that were completely immersed in flames.

The soldiers driving the carriages quickly slowed their horses to a halt, and the women and children immediately poured out of the carriages, running toward the east, as the riders pulled out their bows and arrows, prepared to fight off the blazing beasts.

The woman carrying her baby raced as smoothly as possible so to not harm her baby, hurrying eastward as the crowd of women and children rushed together like a stream running off the end of a cliff.

Cracking of collapsing branches behind them cascaded through the forest as the flock of phoenix plunged into the trees, setting the forest on fire.

To the left of this herd of women and children were more eastern warriors coming into battle. They began to disperse, some staying in this area to fight and protect the women and children, while the others continued on westward to fight the rest of the western army.

The woman carrying her child soon became tired, still not very far from the cart she had fled off of, and began to walk, drained of energy as the flock of phoenix reached the forest floor, torching everything that came close to them, crowing out a high pitched screeching cry.

Somehow, amidst the orchestra of chaotic sounds, the galloping of a single horse riding in the distance from behind the women met her ears, and she turned around to see a man of the eastern army riding in her direction.

As he came closer, she lifted one hand up, waving at him, and calling out for him to stop.

"Stop!" she screamed, jumping in front of the rider upon his horse, giving him no choice than to cease, the horse kicking its front legs into the air, tossing dirt onto the woman.

"I must send word for more warriors!" he yelled at her from his seat on his horse as she blocked his way. "Move away!"

"Take my baby!" she yelled hysterically, lifting her baby up as high as she could, and into his hands, forcing him to take the baby that was now crying loudly, adding to the unbearable sounds of the battle that had begun.

His hands that were covered in cold metal armor cupped the newborn as the baby's mother ran away from the warrior, in hopes that he could save her child.

With not another moment to lose, he held the baby with his right arm, as safely as he could against his armor plated chest, and with his left, continued to guide the horse through the forest, quickly leaving the area.

The eyes of the mother swelled with tears as she watched the forest become engulfed in a furious ocean of flames, the raging smell of sulfur, burning wood, and smoke as black as a starless night in the west, filling the air from all her sides. There was no escape at this point.

Elijah suddenly jolted upward in his bed, quickly waking from the dream he was having. It was a dream that had haunted him since his childhood. He knew what it was, because it was his own past.

Though it was the first days of his existence, nearly sixteen years ago, it was the most vital of the days he had lived. They were days that paved way for his destiny; a plan of hope.

Beads of sweat rolled from his head as his heartbeat began to slow back to a steady rhythm, sinking back into its rightful place in his chest. Wiping his face with his thin woven blanket, he slid back under his bed sheets, laid down once again, and began to stare toward the brick ceiling high above his head, the ceiling hidden beneath the shadows of night, while the dark room that was lit by the moon's beams, which penetrated through the large open balcony, became still again. It had been days since he and his father returned from the meadow, but his deepest anxieties had been rekindled, like brush added to a dying fire, or air returning into emptied lungs.

A brief moment passed by, with a gentle breeze of air flowing into the room. The faint sound of a flute's melody dancing weightlessly on the wind streamed into Elijah's room, meeting his ears, and bringing him peace. Without questioning the music's origin, he fell into a tranquil slumber.

Seth's Courage

Soft echoes of what sounded like blustering thunder rolled through the unbreakable grey fog that filled the air surrounding a king dressed in white and gold plated armor, his young son of eleven years at his side, dressed in a dark green wool tunic. The son was just a little over half the height of his father, and carried his father's wooden bow in his arms. The king gripped with one hand his sword handle, his sword sheathed upon his left thigh, and had an open hand on the back on his son, guiding him alongside his father. Both were uneasy, not knowing what could happen in this foreign land they had travelled into.

Surrounding them were seven guards, walking in a circle around the two royals, all seven with their swords drawn, and shields raised up to their chests. Several feet in front of, and several feet behind the circle of seven guards, walked two of the Diadem, both with their long thin swords drawn as well, but with their shields still strapped to their backs. Never before had the Diadem been so cautious, truly needing to be ready for a fight to defend their king's life.

It was during the reign of King Adam that the first times of betrayal and evil in the east had come to pass. Adam had many sons, his firstborn being Cain, and his second born being Abel. The last few kings who had preceded Adam had begun a trend in which the firstborn son of the king was first in line to be the next crowned king when the time came. When Cain grew to the right age, he expected to begin training with his father to take the throne, but, to his surprise, and the surprise of many, Adam did not do this. Years went by, and Adam did not train Cain, though Cain waited for his training to begin. Instead, at the appropriate time, Adam began to train Abel to take the throne when the time was to come. At these actions, jealousy and rage burned within the heart of Cain, and he secretly began a rebellion in his father's kingdom, amongst the inhabitants of the city, and certain members of the army that Cain had special influence over.

One day, Cain approached his father and demanded that he be next in line to wear the eastern crown, and be made king at the end of his father's reign. In this public outrage, Cain also threatened to kill Abel, his jealously fully taking control of his actions. King Adam, astonished at the audacity of his son's defiance, rebuked him in front of everyone that was in the presence of this confrontation that took place in the throne room, and then revoked Cain's rights as a prince in the eastern kingdom. With bitterness and hatred peaking in Cain's heart, he, and the army of rebels he had conjured up from within the eastern kingdom, all left the east, and set out toward the west, away from the kingdom they had grown to hate. Because of their binding to the royal family, two of the Diadem were forced to follow Cain, and were tossed into shadow, no longer being creations of light, but instead darkness, a reflection of the rebellious heart within Cain.

Adam made a decree to the entire eastern realm, forbidding anyone to come in contact with any of those who had left in rebellion. Even as the banished army marched past the forest settlement on their journey westward, they were ignored, with all the villagers remaining in their homes until the last of the vagabonds had left their area of the forest.

After traveling westward for many days, the rebels came to the end of the forest they had been in their entire time walking, and found they had been led to a large flat desert filled with sand, large boulders, and very little brush. After more walking, they reached the base of a jagged mountain range. It was here that they made a settlement and built a kingdom like their ancestors had in the east, but on a much smaller scale, only being about one-sixth the size. After about a year, the building was complete, and a crown was forged from silver that was found in caves in the mountain range behind the kingdom. Cain crowned himself, and led this kingdom that was filled with liars, thieves, and haters of the eastern kingdom and its ways of righteousness. This new western kingdom was named

Kingdom of Cain. In this same year, Cain crowned a woman as his queen, and in less than a year after that, she gave birth to their son, Enoch.

Though Cain had led a rebellion and began a new kingdom apart from his father, it was still not enough. The hate in his heart was unquenchable, and though several years passed, time did not ease his rage, but instead caused it to intensify.

When Cain had still been living in the east, he would eavesdrop on the teachings Adam had been giving Abel, allowing Cain the ability to have vital knowledge that he eventually passed on to Enoch. Cain taught his son about the great beasts the voice in the sky had banished down to the depths below the earth's surface, and how there were two doorways of onyx that could be opened to release them, one being in the mountains behind the western kingdom.

Soon enough, Cain, Enoch, and the two Diadem bound to this royal bloodline set out to the mountains to search for the low pit that had the onyx seal. Upon finding it, Cain opened the seal, and called forth one of the great beasts of legend that had been banished ages ago. From the opening came a giant beast in the form of a lizard, and as it took its first step onto the earth, a blanket of shadow suddenly developed high in the atmosphere, throwing the entire western realm, as far east as the desert went, into a permanent night time, the moon being the only source of light, with no stars to be seen again. The area where the forest of the east met the desert of the west grew a great fog that split the land in two, and the fog caused the plant life it touched in the forest to die, and the sand it touched in the desert to turn black. Villagers from the settlement in the forest immediately took notice of the great fog, and sent a messenger from their village to the eastern kingdom with word of the strange occurrence.

At once, Cain ordered the massive lizard that stood three times taller than him to go east, and destroy his family's kingdom. Enraged by the boldness this king had to give orders to a beast of such great strength and might, the lizard immediately attacked Cain, his crown falling from his head, landing nearby the open seal, as the lizard picked Cain up with his mouth, and ate him. As this happened, Enoch fled to hide in a nearby cave, hoping the beast would not acknowledge him, and that it would move on. Enoch's attempt was successful, and the beast, ignoring the Diadem, began a journey eastward, prepared to destroy anything and everything it came across. Though they searched for Enoch, the Diadem were unable to find him. Embarrassed by their failure to protect the king and prince, they took the crown, and fled back to the western throne room, placing the fallen king's crown on his seat, awaiting another person to rise to power and take the throne.

Moments after the Diadem left the pit, Enoch walked out, and stood beside a hole left in the earth by the vanished onyx seal. A great sound of eruption was coming from within the pit; the sound of the army of rebels that had been banished by the great thundering voice, racing to the opening to be released from their dungeon beneath the earth's surface. Immediately, Enoch commanded the onyx seal to shut again, and because of his bloodline, the seal had to obey his command. The army of rebels was kept bound beneath the earth's surface, but one of its members was left to wreak havoc in the darkened west. After closing the onyx doorway, Enoch returned to the cave he was hiding in, and was never seen again.

Destruction came to the western kingdom because of the beast. Nearly every building in its city was destroyed, and much of the castle was toppled over. Just as the beast took the life of the western king, it took the life of the western queen, along with most of the west's population. What few survivors there were from the city fled to the mountains to hide in its trails of caves, seeking refuge from the beast, and they, like Enoch, were never seen again.

Soon enough, the eastern kingdom sent a small group of twenty warriors, led by Prince Abel, to investigate the fog, and to see what had caused it. After about two weeks, a single warrior from the group returned, strapped to his stumbling horse, with the warrior barely alive due to many injuries he had received while away from the east.

He told King Adam of the terrible things that had happened in the west that caused the fog barrier, the eternal night, and the death of Cain. Along with these things, the most sorrowful of all the news was that Abel had fallen in battle against the wicked beast.

Great mourning fell over the entire kingdom, especially over King Adam. At a loss of direction for what to do next, Adam went into the sacred garden, and in this place found peace again to lead his followers. He allowed his kingdom to mourn at the loss of their upcoming king for one more day, and at the end of it, named the eastern kingdom, Kingdom of Abel. The day preceding the last of the days of mourning also became a yearly day in which this piece of history was remembered by a large feast in honor of the fallen prince. The kingdom being named, and the yearly feast, were set as memorials for their fallen prince, and were to be a sign that even in the darkest hour, there would still be a hope to come when courage to continue on triumphed over fear. It was a reminder that there would always be hope in the east.

Adam, his two Diadems, seven of his greatest warriors from his army, and his young son, Seth, the next in line to take the throne, then set out to stop the beast in the west before it was to reach the east. The king did not bring his army because he knew that the strength of mere men would not be enough to stop the beast. The only hope at destroying the beast laid in six pieces of a suit of legend that would take years to gather together, so the king, thinking there was not enough time for that, quickly set out to find the beast, and lure it back into its dungeon by opening the onyx seal and shutting it with the beast returned to beneath the earth's surface.

They rode on horses until reaching the muggy fog barrier, and then continued on foot, hoping to be quieter, so to eventually reach the great pit unnoticed, and from there lure the beast to them by drawing its attention.

Pieces of small rocks slowly trickled down the side of the mountain, leaving behind tiny rising clouds of shuffled dust, as the brave group from the east slowly stepped across a narrow pathway, leading towards the base of the mountain, their thick brown boots rubbing against the rocky soil beneath them. They were now traveling in a single file line, while the air stood still in this place, and the faint sound of roaring wind in the distance became audible, though they could not feel it.

One by one, the group of men reached the end of the path, and stepped onto the ground, the sound of roaring wind becoming louder to them as they did, though there was still no wind to be felt blowing. The group, still led by one of the Diadem, continued their march on the ground, winding around a collection of large grey boulders. Suddenly, the moving line came to a halt before it turned the corner of another boulder. The leading Diadem turned around, faced the group following him, and motioned for the king, who was walking at the center of the line, to join him at the head of the line. Adam did this, taking Seth with him, while Adam still held one hand on his sheathed sword and the other on Seth's back. The Diadem turned forward again, motioning for the king to slowly look behind the boulder they were about to pass by, the sound of raging wind now accompanied by a stomping that shook the ground beneath their feet, and a high pitched scratching noise that had no rhythm or pattern to it.

In the slyest of ways, the king peaked from behind the large boulder his men stood behind to see a massive lizard gnawing at a huge disc shaped stone of onyx implanted in the ground at the center of the enormous pit. The scales of this beast were nearly the size of the king's open hand behind his sons back, and were a shade of pink so translucent that the veins and organs of the beast could be visible from its belly. From the back of its neck, leading down across its spine, to the end of its tail, were long spikes that were warped, and sharper than the swords these eastern warriors carried. The source of that deceiving sound that they thought to be wind was the heavy breathing that came from the lizard's long mouth, its sharp faded yellow teeth trying to grasp and twist the onyx doorway, but to no avail, not even leaving behind a scratch, and only creating the high pitched noise the men had heard. Within its mouth was a long dark purple tongue, and from its open mouth dripped out cloudy saliva that emitted a foul odor. Its shiny eyes, about four scales in diameter each, were blood red, with a diagonal shaped pupil of white.

The curled razor sharp claws that came from the lizard's four webbed feet scratched at the earth, which was a mix of pebbles and sand, as the beast used all its might in an attempt to remove the thick seal of precious stone, and release its fellow rebels from their place of torment.

The Diadem at the end of the line walked up beside the prince, and looked to the other Diadem, who silently faced back at him, neither of their eyes having pupils, but instead a solid white glaze over their eyes. They looked back towards the direction of the beast, and gently pulled the king and prince behind them.

In absolute silence and synchronization, the two Diadem bent down to the ground, their feet firmly planted flat, and their folded legs pressed against their chests. They pulled their shields off their backs, and set them, along with their swords, on the ground. They folded in their arms, and spread their elbows out at their sides, bowing their heads to the ground. Their folded legs were then absorbed into their torsos, and their folded arms became whole pieces as their feet shrunk in, and then stretched out again, forming into talons. Their noses began to grow out, and sharply curve down at the end, becoming beaks. Their skin began to grow long feathers, and their arm appendages became long wings. The king and prince looked down to the two Diadem to now see them in the form of white eagles.

The Diadem flapped their wings, the ends of the feathers waving in the air as they did, stirring the air around them, and flew up, above the boulder, toward the lizard. The scratching against the onyx quickly stopped with the two Diadem catching the attention of the lizard, while the group of men remained hidden.

A hideous growl began to vibrate from the lizard's grinding jaw as the Diadem fluttered in the air, leading the lizard's gaze toward the opposite direction of the boulder that was hiding the rest of the group.

The lizard crouched its body low to the ground, as though it were about to pounce up at the Diadem, with its tail pressed against the ground, slowly dragging it back and forth, with every sway of its tail grinding the ground beneath it, causing enough noise for the seven men to pour out into the pit, creating a half-circle along the pit wall behind the unaware beast.

Adam, who was still behind the large boulder with Seth, then crept out into the pit, leaving his son behind, his father's bow still gripped tightly in his hands. With both hands now on his sheathed sword, Adam walked into the opening, drawing close to the slithering tail that was motioning from side to side.

Without warning, the beast's moving tail came to a stop, and the king was frozen in his tracks, not taking another step so to not make a sound and be noticed. Just as the king looked up to the Diadem who were still flying, now directly above the lizard's head that was pointed upward, the lizard leaped up off the ground, snapping its jaws at the Diadem who easily dodged the lizard's mouth. Once the heavy body of the lizard crashed back onto the ground, the entire pit shook, tossing the king and his men into the air, and onto the ground. Adam was thrust forward toward the beast, falling onto the ground that had been churned up by its tail. In reaction to the sound of clanking armor against the ground, the beast whipped its tail, slapping Adam's body, and flung him across the pit. His spinning body landed abruptly onto the onyx seal, and his head slammed onto it roughly, leaving him unconscious.

A deep crackling roar violently rolled out from the lizard's open mouth as it spun around to see the men who had entered the pit, all their swords now raised up, knowing their weapons would do no good, only hoping that their courage would sustain them.

As the giant lizard charged at one of the men, one of the Diadem swiftly swooped down to the king, grabbed onto his shoulders with his talons, and lifted the king into the air, away from the pit. Pieces of the king's armor began to fall off his body as he was taken away, Seth flinching at the sound of each piece hitting the ground, each sound forcing his fears within to fight against his courage.

The warriors struck their swords against the rough exterior of the lizard, but not a dent was left on its iron-like scales. If any of the warriors were to strike at the lizard's body hard enough with his sword, the sword would shatter like fallen glass upon stone ground. The second Diadem that was still in the pit repeatedly dove at the lizard, scratching at the lizard's hide with his talons, but it was still not strong enough to tear through the lizard's scales, though it did leave marks across its back.

Seth watched as one by one, six of the seven warriors fell in battle against the giant lizard that could not be slain. The seventh warrior was at the opposite end of the pit from where Seth watched, his hands and feet shaking in fear, his heart beating at a pace that nearly caused it to burst out from his chest. Splinters began to stab into his fingers as he gripped even more tightly onto his father's bow.

The pulsing of Seth's heart and shaking of his body began to pound in unison, his whole body feeling as though it were to explode from the throbbing at any moment. Replays of his father being knocked down and flown away took hold of his sight, and fear overcame the boy. He was about to be the last one left with this beast that could not be stopped.

Two single tears spilt out from Seth's open eyes as he saw the seventh warrior fall in battle with the lizard.

Within Seth's mind, he came to the realization that if this beast was not stopped, everyone else in the entire Kingdom of Abel would suffer this way, or even more greatly than these men just had. If this beast was not to be stopped now, all these fallen men, and his brother, Abel, would have died in vain. Suddenly, all the fear within Seth that had peaked seemed to vanish, and complete clarity and courage filled every ounce of his being.

"Enough!" Seth yelled, throwing down his father's bow, and running into the open pit, toward the direction of the lizard.

At this, the lizard spun back around toward where the men had first entered the pit, and saw the young prince who had stopped in his tracks, with the onyx seal in the ground about thirty feet in front of Seth. Another fifty feet behind the onyx seal was the lizard that instantly began to charge toward Seth.

In a panic, the Diadem viciously clawed at the racing lizard's back, leaving scratches across several scales, but still not breaking its hide. The lizard ignored this, and continued quickly toward the young prince, its feet pounding into the ground, leaving its claw prints as tracks behind it.

Kneeling to the ground, Seth laid his small open hands onto the sandy earth and looked to the onyx stone that reflected the dim light of the exposed moon that seemed to hover directly above the pit.

"Though I wear no crown, I am royalty," Seth whispered out to the onyx seal, ignoring the slamming steps of the lizard as it neared him, a storm of dust filling the air behind the speeding beast. "Onyx seal, I command you to be opened once again!"

The lizard's eyes, fixed on Seth, craving the life of the prince, did not notice the seal that it was about to run across, though the onyx stone began to faintly glow.

"Be opened!" Seth shouted at the onyx seal as he threw his body back, his fingers piercing into the ground to keep his body propped up, as the lizard fully stepped onto the wide seal that was longer and wider than the beast's body.

At the sound of the prince's command, a brilliant light of white flashed from the onyx seal, so bright it caused Seth to cover his eyes, and once the light vanished, the onyx stone was gone, causing the beast to fall back beneath the earth.

A screeching roar from the beast became an echo as it fell deep within the earth, while the Diadem landed beside Seth. Seth quickly pulled his hands away from his eyes to see the lizard gone, and the seal left open.

"Be shut!" Seth commanded, his eyes burning furiously at the open pit.

With another blinding flash of white light, Seth threw his face down into the grey sand, covering the top of his head with his hands, and the onyx seal returned. Before he could lift himself up again, he felt the talons of the Diadem that had stayed with him wrap around his shoulders, and Seth's body was lifted off of the ground.

The Diadem lifted him high into the air, while Seth picked his hands up, gripping the Diadem's talons, as Seth looked down to the bare and empty mountains while they flew away. From behind the clouds they passed by came the other Diadem, carrying Adam, who was still unconscious, with his crown still firmly planted on his head, and they continued moving eastward to return home. Seth observed the entire western realm as they did, noting the devastation that had come due to the jealousy and hate in his brother's heart. Though the beast had been stopped, and the western kingdom's rebellion was forcefully ended, the aftermath was horrific. The blanket of shadow never lifted, and the entire western realm became a wasteland that all inhabitants of the Kingdom of Abel were forever forbidden to go to.

Reaching the end of the western desert, the Diadem flew the two royals into the fog barrier, remaining at their quick speed, gliding hundreds of feet into the air, high over the dead trees that were now only warped wooden barks and branches. In his heart, Seth knew that he would once again see a time of great war and destruction due to hearts like Cain's, Cain only being the catalyst for far worse rebellions. Cain would only be the first of many to try to rise to power when they were not called to do so, his wicked example leading others to come after him into the deceptive darkness he had drowned in. Seth could feel within him that he would one day, again, have to stand against a similar darkness in a time of hopelessness. Though he was still a young boy, a high level of acceptance had birthed itself in his heart.

His tunic became damp with the fog sinking into his clothing as he glided through the barrier, a slight chill coming over his body.

Within a moment, the flying survivors broke through the fog barrier, and reached open air over the eastern forest, where, above the tree tops the beams of sunlight filled the air. The sun had just begun to rise, bringing the morning of a new day to the east. Seth looked down to the tops of the lush green trees to see a few thin lines of grey smoke slowly streaming out from between the trees, their source being the village of the settlement in the forest. It was in this instance of foresight that Seth found a peace that passed reasoning, because he didn't rely on his own strength to get him through the great hours of shadow that were to return to him one day.

As they glided along the warmth of the air, Seth's eyes moved from the tops of the trees to the furthest east he could see, toward a shimmering light in the distance. The Kingdom of Abel's white stone towers were being struck by the rising sun's rays, reflecting a light that echoed a sound of victory over the entire eastern land. Though an unknown future was soon to play itself out, the sun was still shining brightly from the perspective where Seth was watching from. Seth had never seen the east like this before.

King Seth, nobly standing tall, watched over his kingdom from the flattened area of the castle roof, in front of the sacred garden as the sun was slowly slipping behind the horizon in the west, sinking behind the furthest views of the forest that seemed to slowly be absorbing the massive star. The golden staff that was held upright in the king's hand was reflecting the setting beams of the sun off of it, while the keepers of the torches along the great wall began to travel from torch to torch, refilling the torches with more oil and hay, setting them aflame.

A sudden chilling wind quickly slithered through the air, passing along the bearded cheeks of Seth, quickly catching his attention, as the gust disappeared just as quickly as it had come. An eerie feeling settled over him, forcing his eyes to shift across the flat land, as though he were searching for something that could not be seen, but felt instead. He shut his eyes, and took a deep breath. His lungs took in as much oxygen as they could, and his chest beneath his heavy royal robes expanded outward.

His chest began to deflate as he breathed out, releasing all his air, and then opening his eyes, his vision fixed on the sun setting in the west. His eyes burned ferociously as he saw past what he could not see, staring into the west.

"A familiar shadow is waking in the west," Seth softly whispered from his chapped lips that were hidden beneath his frizzy white beard.

Seth slowly turned his back on the west, and took seven steps forward, walking up to the silver entrance doors of the sacred garden. He reached out his left hand, gripped onto the circular door handle that was implanted on the door at about the height of his chest, and pulled the door toward him, opening it.

Seth quickly entered the garden, and shut the door behind him.

Olivia's Rebellion

"There is a threat to your kingdom," an elderly witch draped in torn rags of black declared as she stood over a pile of coals that were burning, releasing streams of maroon and dark green smoke up to her hidden face that was covered by a long hanging hood.

Behind her stood five more witches dressed exactly like her, only lacking the red rope tied around the waist of the witch who spoke. These five remained frozen still in the dimly lit throne room of the Kingdom of Cain, their bodies like statues left for decoration.

"Continue to tell me what you see," the queen of the west, Olivia, commanded from her throne of carved silver, as the witches stood at the bottom of the set of the six steps that led up to the throne she occupied.

Moonlight peered into the dark room through red and clear stain-glass windows, the dim light accompanied by torches lit along the wall, keeping the room dark, hiding within it the secrets of

Olivia's trickery and plotting. The coolness of the air combated against the warmth of the queen's breath, creating streams of fog to slither from her shiny lips as she spoke. At the queen's feet sat her two Diadem in the form of large black panthers, their throats vibrating as they purred contently beneath her. Their lengthy tails whipped back and forth, and their heads were facing the witch that stood closest to the queen, with their solid and intimidating red eyes focused on her.

"A threat is coming," the witch continued to explain in her scratchy voice, looking into the smoke, seeing the future with her gift of foresight that was fueled by the darkness in the west, a power known to be wicked by those in the east. "A threat to your kingdom is coming in the form of a man who will come from the forest settlement in the west. He will be born soon, this boy who you have a connection to. In the forest of the east, a prince will be born, and he will destroy you if he is allowed to mature into a man. Destroy him as an infant, or he will surely bring the downfall of your reign in the west."

"There is no royal family in the forest!" the queen loudly interrupted, challenging the accuracy of this prophecy.

"He will inherit the crown your heart has longed after," the witch went on. "He will lead armies against you, and the Kingdom of Cain. He is the threat I see."

"I should be the ruler of that kingdom," the queen screamed, standing from her throne, closing her hands into tight fists. "Not some peasant from the forest! If I am to send an army, will I be able to successfully destroy the entire population of the forest village, especially the boy you speak of? Where exactly is he?"

"Yes," the witch replied, the smoke pouring into her hood that had thread dangling all around its rim. "You will succeed. But send many armies, because the king of the east, your father, has already foreseen this battle you ask of, and is preparing to send his eastern army to the forest. But, my queen, I am certain you will have the power to overcome his armies in battle. As for the boy, I cannot find his exact location. He is in the darkness of his mother's womb where I am blind to. But I see him being crowned king, if he is not killed as a baby. He is not like most others from the forest village; there is something different about him, but I cannot see what it is. And there is another boy of significance, the same age as the boy from the forest, but this second boy is in the city of the eastern kingdom, though I can't see his exact location either. He is tied to the boy in the forest somehow, nearly as much as you are, but I cannot see why either. I only know it will not be until much later that he will play a vital part in all this, and his importance is dependent on the first boy's survival."

The witch speaking began to cough, and stumbled onto the ground, grasping onto the rough red carpet beneath her that led up to Olivia's throne.

"I am drained of energy," she coughed out from beneath her

hood. "I have seen too far into the future for my powers to remain strong and of good use. The more I look, the less I see. I must rest now."

"You other witches," Olivia announced to the five behind the main one that was speaking, "tend to your mother. See to it that she is prepared to speak to me again upon my return from the eastern forest. I will heed her council, and go into battle immediately."

The witch standing in the middle of the row floated up to the main witch, holding tongs in one hand, and a bucket in the other. She leaned over, picked up the burning coals with the rusty tongs, and placed them in the bucket, as the other four glided up to their mother, helped her up, and began to glide away from the platform that Olivia's throne rested on, toward the exit.

"Generals!" Olivia called out as her two head generals over the western army stepped out from the shadows before the throne steps. "Assemble my entire military force. We will leave within the next few hours to destroy the people of the forest, and the entire forest itself as we pass through it. Inform your men that nothing we come across is to survive, whether it be plant, animal, or man."

"And know this," Olivia redirected her voice, pointing a finger to the witches who were about to exit her throne room, "if you spoke lies to me, and I lose this battle against my father's kingdom, it will be your lives I will take next."

During the reign of King Seth, he and his wife, Mary, gave birth to only one child: their daughter, Olivia. Though Seth and Mary longed for more children, especially a son to take the crown from Seth at the appointed time, Mary never again became pregnant. Because she had no siblings, Olivia thought that she would be the first lead queen to rule over the east, but it was against the leading of the voice that roared like thunder for this to happen. When Olivia reached the age that the princes before her began their training to be kings, she, and many in the kingdom, anticipated her training to begin, but, like with her uncle, Cain, the training did not come. Years went by, and the same bitterness and hate that was birthed in Cain's heart began to churn in Olivia's, foaming over with rebellious thoughts against her father. As Olivia grew in age, she walked in the same steps as her uncle, Cain, secretly gathering other rebellious souls within the Kingdom of Abel to form an army for her to lead.

One day, in the throne room of King Seth, Olivia approached her father, demanding that she take the crown from him at the end of his reign, since he had no other children to give it to. Enraged at her defiance and rebellious mindset toward what he was doing in accordance with the One's instructions, he banished her to the west. So, Olivia gladly left, her assembled army revealing themselves as the rebels they were, following behind her as she marched away from the Kingdom of Abel. Before the last rebel even walked outside of the city walls, a decree was instated, by Seth, saying that these rebels were never to be aided or spoken to by anyone from the east. Full of pride and hatred, the group marched onward to the ruins of the Kingdom of Cain.

Upon their trek through the forest, passing by the forest settlement, every occupant of the village closed themselves away, ignoring the rebels passing by, showing no remorse or compassion for these haters of the east.

Olivia, and her army, repaired the destroyed Kingdom of Cain within two years, and remained there, under the covering shadow in the sky, never again stepping into the light of day. Olivia took up the crown of her uncle, and the two dark Diadem were then bound to her. The kingdom in the west once again became home to liars, thieves, rebels, and those who hated the east, though not nearly as much as their queen. Though given her own kingdom, she still longed for the crown of the east, and for vengeance against those she felt had wronged her. History repeated itself, from one generation to the next, and with it, the continuation of the war against the east.

"Where is she?!" Olivia screamed from her silver throne, slamming her closed fists against the throne's arm rests, with the five daughters of the witch that foresaw a threat to Olivia's kingdom in chains standing before her. "Where is your mother who spoke lies to me?"

"She has disappeared," one of the five hooded women hissed.

"Then I will order every last person in my kingdom to find her," Olivia announced to the five who were trembling in fear at what was to happen to them. "And she will be punished as I warned she'd be. Until she's found, your lives will suffice. Remove them from my castle."

A young boy, that was about the age of ten, stepped out from his post along the wall. He grabbed one end of the chains, yanked it, and pulled the group of five behind him as he walked them out of the throne room, heading for the center of the city where the five would be stoned.

This was the day that Olivia returned from her battle against the east in which she attacked the village in the forest. Her entire army had been destroyed in battle, being consumed by the earth, and so she had called for every male child and man not yet in the military, in the west, to begin training as warriors to replace their fallen fathers and brothers, and become Olivia's new army.

The foresight her servant had given her that led Olivia into battle had been wrong, and so she was prepared to put this witch to death. A fresh hatred for her father brewed within her, but the fact that the entire village in the forest, and its residents, had been completely destroyed brought enough relief to keep her from any sudden or drastic attempts at attacking the eastern kingdom. It was to her knowledge that no survivors were left in the wake of the devastation.

"It's nearly sixteen years to the day that I lost my entire army," Olivia reminisced as she sat on her silver throne, speaking to

Oliver, the captain over her current army, which was now extremely large and powerful.

"Yes," the captain responded, "I remember being only a child, and dragging the five daughters of the hag to be stoned at the town center."

"They paid greatly for their mother's disappearance," Olivia chuckled, her Diadem perched on the top of her throne in the form of ravens. "Though she was never found, I feel a worse fate befell her."

The entrance doors to the throne room were shut, with Olivia, Oliver, and the Diadem alone in the large room. Fiery light from the hundreds of candles on the wall behind her throne lit up the room, as a plan of utmost secrecy began to unfold.

"It's time," Olivia whispered, stretching out her hands, and sticking out her pointer fingers as perches for her obedient Diadem to land on. "I've waited nearly sixteen years for this moment."

From above the queen's sight fluttered down two black moths that landed on her fingers, one on her left, the other on her right, their wings presenting swirling black patterns that looked like giant eyes. These moths were the Diadem that were ravens just a moment before.

"The western military will be notified to assemble before we return from the pit," Oliver spoke, his voice shaky. "…If we return."

"Do you question my plan?" Olivia quickly responded to him, flicking her left pointer finger, thrusting the Diadem off of her finger, and at Oliver.

While in midair, the wings of the moth quickly rolled up, wrapping around its own body, and then began to stretch out, scales forming from its silky wings. As its scaling body stretched out, it grew thick, and the head of a snake formed at one end of the body, beady red eyes opening above fangs that popped out of its formed mouth, speedily growing ten feet long. Once it landed onto Oliver, it quickly wrapped its muscular body around him, binding his arms at his side, and holding his legs from moving. Oliver fell to the ground as the serpent tightened its grip with every one of his exhales. The veins on Oliver's neck swelled up as he looked up at Olivia in a panic, his entire body feeling as though it were caving in on himself, with his bones only moments from breaking.

"Forgive me," Oliver managed to painfully speak in an airy voice, his scrunched up face turning from a shade of red to violet.

At his plea, the Diadem quickly unraveled itself from Oliver's body and slithered back to Olivia. Oliver coughed, grabbing at his throat, air rushing back into his emptied lungs, like rain falling from a vengeful storm cloud.

"Oliver, don't think I won't take your life too, if you are to get in my way, even by means of your doubt," Olivia growled at him as the slithering Diadem slid up onto Olivia's lap, balling up as though to take a nap, her left hand lowering itself to pet the damp snake. "It won't be like the way it was when my uncle opened the onyx seal and released a beast from the world beneath our feet. He was weak, and a fool. I will simply persuade the same beast to join the west in revenge against the east. I'm sure it has been waiting to revisit the one who threw it back beneath the earth once it had already been set free."

Micah's Destiny

"My queen," Mareshah, one of the generals of the eastern armies called out, entering the throne room of the palace of the Kingdom of Abel, carrying in his arms a ball of purple cloth.

His deep voice calling out to Queen Mary was accompanied by the sounds of a baby crying, and the clanking of the heavy metal armor that he was wearing. Behind him, the entrance doors were quickly shut, leaving him alone with the queen, and her head maidservant, inside the tall throne room.

Queen Mary, sitting upon her large glass throne that sat at the left hand of the larger throne that was carved from opal, which the king sat on, began to squint her eyes, magnifying the wrinkles across her cheekbones. She looked to the man who was walking down the long carpet that led to the steps of the platform where the thrones were placed. Night had fallen over the kingdom, and the flames from the torches in the room were not enough to allow the queen to clearly see what the man was carrying.

"Where is that crying coming from?" the queen questioned her maidservant that stood to her left, who was wearing a dull brown dress with a white apron hung over her front side.

"I believe the general is carrying something more than just rags," she replied to the queen, the two women looking down to Mareshah's folded arms.

"My queen," Mareshah spoke again, reaching the steps before the thrones of the royal family, "we reached the village in the forest, but the armies of the west were too close for us to begin to evacuate the village successfully."

"What child is this?" Mary asked, pointing at the baby that was now visible to her, wrapped in purple rags, the queen's hand motions signaling for her maid to take the baby from the general, and deliver it into the queen's hands.

"We were able to reach the village in the forest just before the western army arrived," Maresha began telling the story to the queen as the baby was brought to her.

The baby was traded into Mary's arms, and she cradled him warmly, causing the baby to fall silent as the general continued his story.

"We were able to send out most of the women and children on carriages just in time," the heavily breathing general went on, "but, moments after they departed, the opposing armies reached the village, and we were not strong enough to push back their forces. I returned here, to the Kingdom of Abel, to call for more warriors to go to fight. On my way here, I saw that the wagons carrying the women and children had been abandoned because western enemy forces had reached them. As I passed by them, a woman caused me to stop, handed to me this child, and fled. I had no choice but to continue on to call for more warriors, bringing this baby with me."

"Where are the women and children that evacuated now?" the queen worriedly questioned Maresha, as the maid stood silent, shocked at his story.

"None made it out of the forest," he answered in the silence of the room.

"How many survivors from the forest village are there?" Mary asked another question, hoping to have a less grim answer.

"One," Maresha said, looking to the baby that Mary held dearly.

She looked down at the baby, her old and tired face to his fresh new one, ages separating them, yet drawn close together by her compassion for the orphaned baby. Her hazel eyes began to swell, like a glass having too much drink poured into it, set to overflow, as she looked back to Maresha.

"Were more warriors sent to battle?" she enquired, avoiding her natural emotion to cry over the great loss of the people of the forest, and the great miracle of the baby's survival, maintaining her image of nobility and authority.

"Yes," he told her, the only sounds in the throne room being their voices, and the crackling fire baring light from the torches that smoothly burned upward.

"King Seth set out for the battle site earlier this evening," the queen informed the general. "Return to your family and rest tonight, since today was the Day of Feast, in remembrance of Prince Abel, but, by sunrise, make sure to return for the battle in the forest."

"Pardon my interjection, my dear queen, but it is no longer a battle," the general said, a chill striking the atmosphere, "it has become a war."

At this, Maresha bowed, and turned away, leaving the throne room, as Mary looked back to the baby.

"Shall I take him for you?" the maid asked Mary from the same place she was originally standing.

"No," Queen Mary softly replied, entranced by the baby, "I desire to hold him longer."

Silence once again fell over the throne room as the doors shut with Mareshah leaving, but it was quickly interrupted by Mary's whispers.

"For so long now I have longed for another child, and now in my arms I hold a child that is in need of a mother, and a father, just as well," Mary softly spoke.

The beating heart of Mary became in sync with the baby's, and a peace fell over the both of them, as Mary gently hummed a song that had been passed down from generation to generation in the eastern kingdom, since the reign of the first king: Psalm of the East.

"Let faith guide your steps and hope guard your heart," Mary then began to softly sing the lyrics of the song to the baby. "May peace bring you rest, as light binds the dark. From the sky comes our King, our hope in the east. He'll shelter us all, our worries He'll ease. There's hope in the east."

The heavy reddened eyelids of the porcelain skinned baby gently lifted up, and his two sea-blue eyes that told tales of storm-battered waves peered directly into Mary's eyes, which were swelling with tears that fell onto the dirty purple rags covering the baby, absorbing into the material. As they stared into each other's eyes, a deep connection began to form, as though their essences were pouring into one another, their two paths becoming one, and with this, Mary said her final words for the night.

"He will be my son."

"Father!" six boys exclaimed at different times, running to the doorway of their small house as their father carried himself inside, wearing armor that was weighing him down, and tiring him faster.

His exposed hands felt the tops of his young sons' heads, his fingers running through their thin straight hair, as they surrounded and embraced him, the tallest of his sons not reaching higher than his waist.

"Where is your mother?" he asked them, looking toward the entrance of the hallway that led to the bedrooms, expecting to see his wife to walk out from the hall.

"She's in your room," his oldest son answered, grabbing his father's hand, his brothers grabbing onto their father's armor, and together pulling him toward the closed door to the room where his wife was.

The boys all quickly became silent as they reached the door, one gently pushing it open, and inside was their mother lying on a small bed, with a single candle lit in the windowless room. Within her arms was a ball of bed sheets that she held tightly against her chest.

"Boys," the father softly spoke to his sons, seeing the bundle in his wife's arms, "wait for me outside the room. Your mother needs some rest and quiet."

Obediently, the boys silently trotted out the room, their father shutting the door behind them, and in seconds, their voices and laughter could be heard as they played with each other, excited that their father was home, and eager to hear his stories from the battle he was returning from, only to return to in the morning.

"It's a boy," his wife whispered, lying against the backboard of the bed, her lower half beneath a thick sheet of wool, as her husband walked to the bedside, and sat on its edge.

"Another son," he replied proudly, yet in a meek manor, as he looked into the bundle she held to see the exposed wrinkled face of his new child, still, as he slept in the warm wrapping.

"He was born last night," she continued as he looked to her, their eyes both glistening in the candlelight, "and you have returned. The battle must be over."

"It's far from being over," he told her, his voice sounding drained. "I can only stay the night. The queen ordered I return to the battle tomorrow. I only came back to the kingdom to call for the rest of the army."

"Mareshah," the wife spoke, putting one of her hands on his as their son lay against her chest, now supported by one arm, "will the western armies be reaching us?"

"They do not intend to," he began to explain as the light of the candle flickered, making the shadows on the wall dance. "They were ordered to destroy the people of the forest, but I am not sure why. We were fighting to save them."

"Were they brought to the kingdom safely?" she asked him hopefully.

"Only one," he said grimly, "he was only about the age of this son you hold. I left as the western armies reached their village, but I know in my heart that aside from the single baby, there were no survivors. On my way back to call for more warriors, his mother stopped me, and forced me to take her baby. Once I reached the palace, I gave him to the queen. I suppose he is the last of his people."

"I wouldn't wish for any child to grow up without their parents," she said, holding her son even tighter against her chest.

"Enough of this discussion," Mareshah told his wife, setting his free hand upon the bundled baby, "there are less mournful things to speak of. Have you thought of a name?"

"I want to name him Micah," she said gladly to her husband.

"Micah," he said being able to smile through all the darkness the kingdom was facing. "My seventh son."

That night would be the final night Mareshah would have with Micah, and the rest of his family. Upon returning to the warzone, he became a casualty of the fight. His family was left devastated, and the boys grew up without a father. Micah, being the youngest, was known to be the runt of the seven brothers, and in addition to being trained to be a skillful warrior in battle, he trained himself to play different musical instruments that were commonly played in the Kingdom of Abel.

In the first year of his warrior training, at the age of seven, many people claimed to have heard strange noises outside the kingdom walls. As this happened, people leaving from within the city to the forests to gather food reported seeing a hooded woman that appeared to be from the west. Guards were posted outside the city walls to find her so that she could be captured and possibly punished for coming back to the east if she really was from the west.

"She has been caught!" a man's voice shouted as a parade of people walked quickly through the streets, being led by a guard posted along the kingdom walls, dressed in his plated armor, who was dragging behind him a woman bound with ropes, with her wrists tied together.

Whaling like an injured animal, the witch, completely covered in her black rags, with a red rope tied as a belt at her waist, only exposing the shriveled white skin of her hands and wrists, tossed her body around, fighting to be let loose, hoping to escape her coming judgment. She screamed out as though she were in pain, though none of her words could be understood.

"The witch!" Micah's fourth oldest brother shouted, pointing toward the crowd of people that were walking down the street, soon to pass by the seven boys who were outside the front of their house.

Micah stood frozen, fear filling him, as he saw the witch thrashing her bound hands and kicking her legs, her body being drug across the road by the guard, as they were coming in Micah's direction.

"What is the commotion?" Micah's mother called out, walking out the open door of their house to see the crowd of people nearing, finding her spot to stand behind Micah, her hands on his boney shoulders.

"They caught the witch!" one of her sons shouted as the crowd following the witch reached the front of their house, passing by it as they marched on to the castle.

Just as the witch's covered body passed by Micah, the witch turned her concealed face in his direction, and he stared directly back at her, fear and uncertainty pouring from his eyes.

"You!" she screamed out, causing the crowd to quickly fall silent and the man dragging her to stop in his tracks, while she pointed a shriveled finger at Micah. "You are the boy I could not see all those years ago."

"Be silenced!" the guard that had been dragging her ordered, about to continue his march, but not before striking at the witch's back with a long wooden rod he was carrying.

"Wait," the witch continued beginning to fall into a trance beneath her rags. "I sense him. The one that should be killed first...he's alive! The boy is alive! And you...you must be killed!"

A sudden burst of strength filled the witch as she pulled against the ropes that bound her, pulling hard enough to force the guard to let go, and the witch lunged at the boy.

His mother, her hands still on his shoulders, quickly backed away, puling Micah with her. Just as they moved back, the witch reached out her hand, striking at the front of the boy's right leg, scratching it with her sharp, uncut nails.

Micah immediately let out a cry of pain, still being pulled away by his mother, as the guard got a hold on the rope again, and pulled the witch away from Micah's reach.

"Ah!" Micah yelled, jumping up in his bed, knocking away heavy sheets that were piled over him.

"Micah," the brother he was nearest to in age groaned from the other side of the room, turning over onto his right side to face Micah, as they both lay in their own beds. "This is the fourth night in a row. Is it that nightmare, again?"

"Yes," Micah answered, soft spoken, still shaking from the fear his reoccurring nightmare had left him with.

"It was year's ago," his brother continued, "and we were so young. I don't understand how you could remember it so clearly."

"It's as clear in my mind as the scar she left on my leg," Micah said, his hands stroking the scar on his right leg that was placed just under his kneecap.

"Well, even still," his brother argued, "that witch was stoned that day for being in the east, and with her death all her curses were reversed."

"What she said was so confusing," Micah responded, desiring to talk about his nightmare, as he frequently managed to with this brother. "What business would she have had seeing me with her witchcraft before she ever met me? And who was the one that should be killed first?"

"For years you have asked that question, and every time you've asked I have given you the same answer: she was speaking nonsense, Micah." His brother reassured him, easing Micah's fears. "She was only trying to scare you. Were you to be destined for anything more than a common warrior in our military, her words would carry weight, but you're not. Now go back to sleep. We've got our special training tomorrow with Jeremiah to look forward to. Let's not keep looking to the past."

Jeremiah was the oldest of the seven brothers in Micah's family. After his father's death, he had vowed to become the greatest of all the warriors in the eastern kingdom. The seeds of determination he sowed through the years returned to him as a harvest of honor. He had become the fiercest warrior of the entire army, and was given authority as captain over all the army. Though there was only peace for the kingdom since the time that Jeremiah became a warrior, it was the king's orders that he would lead the army if there ever were a time of war.

Micah pulled himself out of bed, still unsettled. He bent beneath his bed, raised on blocks at each corner, reaching his hand around until he felt his favorite wooden flute laying on the cold stone floor.

Walking out of his family's house, the flute in his hand, he climbed onto large wooden crates that sat along the side of his brick home, and pulled himself up onto the roof of his house.

The stars were shining brightly this night, high above the calm and quiet kingdom, as if guarding the east from the black sky they were holding up. The lightest of breezes purred through the air, cooling the night even more, soothing Micah's sensitive skin over his extremely thin body.

Micah looked up to the sky, feeling as though he was the only one in the entire eastern realm that was still awake at this hour. He lifted the finely carved flute to his thin lips, and began to play a soft melody that complimented the beauty of the night's reign. The notes he played were of the song that Mary had sung to Elijah over fifteen years ago, and they seemed to glide along the wind, being carried off as far up as to the castle that stood over the city, to its east. Micah found himself at ease again as he played the melody of this tranquil night..

Plague Released

"We have almost arrived!" Oliver shouted to Olivia, the two of them riding on the back of the Diadem that were in the form of giant black crows, Oliver's voice being challenged by the howling wind and distance between him and Olivia. "Behind this last row of mountains is the pit where we'll find the onyx seal!"

Flying over the last mountain top before reaching the gap in the middle of the mountain range, Olivia looked down to see a great pit surrounded by large boulders, and, at the center of the pit, saw the onyx seal, shimmering like a still pond in the moonlight that was beaming off of its surface.

Gliding down into the pit, Olivia and Oliver's hands gripped onto the feathers of the crows as they descended, while a thin and slowly moving stream of smoke climbing up from a corner of the pit caught Olivia's gaze.

"Take me to the source of that smoke," Olivia commanded the

Diadem she rode on, causing it to land away from the center of the pit, with Oliver and his Diadem following behind them.

Once the crow landed on the ground, Olivia slid off of it, and walked up to what looked like the remains of a small fire that had just been put out. Water was still puddled over and around the pile of broken pieces of burnt wood and charred weeds.

"We're not alone," Oliver spoke, now on foot, as he caught up to the queen and her discovery, quickly pulling out his sword, and turning to face the boulders circling the pit. "Who goes there?"

From the shadows furthest away from him appeared a set of eyes that radiated a bright shade of red, penetrating the darkness around it, but giving light to nothing else.

"Show yourself!" Olivia ordered as she came up beside Oliver who was fixed on the eyes. "As Queen of the West, I demand you show yourself!"

Breaths passed, and there was no response from the floating red eyes. While Oliver and Olivia remained still where they stood, Oliver's sword stretched out in front of him, ready to strike if attacked.

"The west has no queen!" a deep voice defiantly sounded from where the red eyes floated. "The crown you wear means nothing to me."

"How dare you!" Olivia roared, turning to her two Diadem, but as she did, the floating red eyes disappeared, and the sound of feet racing along the sandy ground softly echoed, too soft for the group from the western kingdom to hear from where they stood. "Kill him!"

The Diadem, now in the shape of men, ran toward where the red eyes were, but didn't find a trace of anything there. Olivia and Oliver quickly walked up to where the Diadem stood perplexed, unable to figure out where the mysterious creature vanished to.

"This is some type of trickery," Oliver growled, thirsty for a fight. "Was it a rogue witch, perhaps? Nobody has been seen in these mountains for decades."

"It doesn't matter anymore," Olivia hissed, turning toward the center of the pit, and stomping her way toward the onyx stone, infuriated by the words of the mysterious creature. "No matter what that creature says or thinks, I am the queen. I alone am the royal of the west; there is no other. I, alone, have the power."

Arriving at the divine onyx stone, Olivia looked down to it. The reflection of the moon could be seen on its perfectly carved surface, this precious stone like no other she had ever seen in the land, its glistening black surface also reflecting the dark blanket hung over the west, amplifying the hue of the onyx.

"It's beautiful," Olivia spoke under her breath, entranced by the beauty of the seal that held the most hideous of creatures beneath it.

She knelt down beside the onyx seal, and set her hand upon its smooth cold surface, overwhelmed by the stone that was not from this earth, while Oliver and the Diadem stood four steps behind her, watching their queen's actions. Before Oliver could realize it, the Diadem had turned back into large crows, returning to the appearance they had when they first landed.

"Though I long to look upon you longer, onyx seal, be removed now." Olivia spoke to the precious stone, causing the same flash of light her father saw as a child to occur, replacing the onyx seal with an open way into the tunnel.

Olivia quickly moved back a few feet from the opening, as a massive, sticky, purple tongue, that was long and thick, began to flap about over the edge of the pit, coming from the darkness within it, and with that, the Diadem lifted into the sky, grabbing Olivia and Oliver, their talons wrapping around their shoulders, pulling the two above the ground of the pit, away from potential danger. The Diadem had clear memory of what happened the last time they had traveled to this pit. They would not let the same fate meet the two they had brought this time.

"I have freed you!" Olivia called down to the pit. "Come forth, beast from the depths. I have need of you."

Long razor claws attached to a large lizard palm lifted up from the pit, and slammed onto the earth's surface, latching onto the edge of the hole that had been opened. Following the hand came the head of a lizard in right proportion to the size of the hand, its scales pink as though it had never seen the light of day, with long and thin spikes across its back that wound like unclipped fingernails. This was the beast that had eaten Cain.

"Return, seal," Olivia quickly muttered from the sky once the lizard fully came out of the pit.

The lizard quickly turned back to the reappeared seal, and began to slam its huge claws against it, infuriated at its return.

"Do you desire to free your brothers?" Olivia shouted down at the lizard, safely out of its reach.

The lizard swung its head toward the four flying in the sky.

"I can help you free them," Olivia spoke to the horrifying beast again, "and I wish to do so for such an honorable beast as you, so mighty and powerful."

"You wear the crown that belonged to one of my meals last I was on this earth's surface," the lizard roared in a disgustingly deep voice, as though mixed with the croaking of a frog, and the cawing of a crow. "Will you follow the same path as its previous owner, and find an end in the grave of my belly?"

"I am not like its previous owner." Olivia continued to attempt to manipulate the beast. "He didn't recognize the strength that you have. I have released you to make a request of you, but not before I was given the privilege to look upon such a magnificent beast that was wrongly imprisoned."

"What request do you have for Plague?" the lizard questioned, revealing its name.

"The followers of the one who imprisoned you have been deserted," Olivia announced to Plague, winning his attention quickly. "The thundering voice no longer dwells among them. He has returned to his throne from where even you once stood before. His earthly followers live in the east, in the Kingdom of Abel. Just as the voice banished you, his followers banished me, into eternal darkness, away from the light of day. I ask that you join me, and seek revenge upon the east, leaving it in utter ruin, so that they receive the due penalty for their actions against us, and even so the King they are waiting to come one day will have no throne to sit on, or kingdom to rule over."

"I will do this," Plague answered the queen, impressed by the focused evil within her, "but you must then also free my brothers from the prison beneath this onyx stone."

"I agree to this," Olivia spoke as the Diadem glided to the ground, still cautious of the unpredictable monster, "but you must first take the life of the king in the east. He is the one who, as a boy, returned you to the darkness of the caverns below, those many years ago."

The enormous lizard thrust open its mouth, and let out a hideous roar that was heard all across the land, both east and west, proclaiming the hatred this beast had for Seth.

"He will share the same end as his brother!" Plague cried out, his hands scratching at the ground, tail whipping against the earth, delight filling Olivia's eyes.

"Then let us return to my western kingdom, and prepare to annihilate the eastern realm," Olivia joyfully told Plague, completely blinded by her own hatred.

"This day, we celebrate the life of the fallen one, my brother, Prince Abel!" King Seth loudly spoke to the city from the balcony overlooking his kingdom from where he made his announcements.

The entire population of the city filled the roads and sidewalks in front of the castle, food and drink all around, as they were prepared to celebrate the yearly Day of Feast. Each one of them had a glass in hand, respectfully listening as the king spoke from the balcony, Mary and Elijah standing at his sides. Though everyone knew Elijah was their son, they did not know he was a survivor from the forest. Rumors and ideas of him being adopted had developed over the years because Mary had never shown to be pregnant before his birth, but it was never spoken of publicly. It was kept secret as best as possible to protect Elijah from danger.

"May his bravery, and courage, forever be remembered!" Seth pronounced mightily, the crowd beneath him yelling cheerfully at his statement, like the sound of waves on the shore. "No matter how dark the night may be, the sun will always be sure to rise."

"Let faith guide your steps, and hope guard your heart," Mary began to sing Psalm of the East, as was tradition for this day, with the entire city immediately joining her in song. "May peace bring you rest, as light binds the dark. From the sky comes our King, our hope in the east. He'll shelter us all, our worries He'll ease. There's hope in the east."

"We will always have hope in the east," Seth smiled, recalling a childhood memory he would never forget, as he and the entire city silently raised their glasses up to the sky. "This hope will unite us at journey's end, in a city of light, where we'll shine as one, you and I. …Let us now drink from our cups, and begin the feast!"

With that being said, silence fell over the city as all the people lowered their glasses to their lips, taking a sip of their drinks, and in that moment, the fierce echoing roar that Plague had let out, from the pit in the west, filled the ears of everyone in the east, rolling over them like an ocean wave tossed in a storm, startling many, leaving them to spill their drinks on themselves. Confusion fell over the people, all of them unsure of the source of the disgusting sound, as they looked to each other, questioning what they had just heard. Their eyes were drawn off of Seth.

Eyes widened, and his drink spilt into his beard from when he shook at the sudden sounding roar, Seth lowered his cup to his side, loosened his grip, and dropped it onto the ground. He looked past the forest beyond the kingdom walls, and his eyes became fixed westward. Stomach churning with fright, and feet frozen in fear over what he knew had been woken in the deep western pit, Seth found himself paralyzed by the coming terror he had waited for since he was flown back from the west.

"Seth," Mary fearfully said, quickly turning to him, "what was that sound? What is happening?"

"We may now feast," Seth quickly yelled to the people, snapping back into reality, bringing the people's attention back to the celebration, forgetting the sound they had just heard.

"Seth," Mary said again, trying to get his attention, while the people returned to the celebration.

Seth spun around, quickly walked off of the balcony, and entered back into the castle, not even realizing that Mary was speaking to him because his attention was fully on what he always knew would return to haunt him.

"Jeremiah," Seth called to the captain who, along with his team of five generals, was standing in the room that led to the balcony that Seth was exiting from, "come with me at once."

As Seth and Jeremiah walked out of the room, and into a closed off room for privacy, Elijah watched them from the balcony, his heart stirring with fear, but his thoughts even more so with curiosity.

"Assemble the army on this solemn day?" Jeremiah surprisingly asked Seth as they stood in the small room with the door shut, leaving the two completely alone.

"Yes," Seth responded, his arms folded behind his back, while his royal staff lay on the tall wooden table at the center of the room beside him and Jeremiah. "That echoing noise that we heard was not the sound of anything that originated from this earth. My own ears have heard it before, and that sound has been seared into my memory since when I first heard it."

"It could not be," Jeremiah gasped, realizing that Seth was referring to the beast that had taken Abel's life: Plague. "Does this mean that the western queen has been destroyed?"

"Most likely," Seth breathed mournfully, pulling his left hand over his face, his palm wiping sweat and worry from his countenance. "Cain did not remain standing before the beast, so I cannot see how Olivia would have a differing outcome."

"We must take Elijah to the pit," Jeremiah quickly advised. "He is young and much stronger than you now in your old age. He is the only one capable of opening and closing the onyx seal."

"Jeremiah," Seth was forced to confess to Jeremiah, "Elijah is not my son by birth. Your father, himself, rescued Elijah as a newborn in the battle against the village in the forest. He brought him to our kingdom, and Elijah has been cared for as our son ever since. He does not carry within him the royal bloodline."

"I suppose I always knew this," Jeremiah admitted, revealing his insight into the matter. "From remembering what my father had spoken to me as a child, that night he returned to the east during the battle in the forest, to talk around the kingdom."

"It has been kept a secret for his safety," Seth explained to the leader of his military. "Were Olivia to know he survived, who knows what lengths she would go to in order to find and kill him, much less now that he is to inherit the crown she has lusted after her entire life."

"I understand." Jeremiah spoke wisely, knowing the importance of keeping Elijah's true origin a secret. "So how can we shut this seal again?"

"Besides Olivia and myself, there is no other person who carries the royal bloodline in their veins," Seth answered, returning back to the task at hand. "Olivia is the only one unaccounted for who has authority over the onyx seals. If she has been killed, which we must assume, only I can shut it again. But, once this beast has been returned to the depths, no future generation will have to deal with these horrors, because once I have passed away, nobody will have the ability to open these seals again. The seals will be unable to be opened, and the wicked rebels will forever be shut beneath the surface of our land. Elijah will take the throne, and replace our bloodline that was first corrupted by my brother's hatred."

"But how will we stop this beast?" Jeremiah questioned the king, still barely able to believe what was happening.

"We will drive him back into the pit from where he came," Seth said, slamming his tightened fist against the wooden table, causing his staff to shake. "We will wait for him in the meadow where we last fought the west. Once the beast breaks through the fog barrier, we will take his attention, and lead him back to the pit. There, I will open the seal, and he will be returned to the darkness."

"My king," Jeremiah quickly responded, "this will be too dangerous for you. There must be another way."

"No!" Seth quickly interrupted. "There is no one else who can remove the seal. I must do this."

"What if you are to fall?" Jeremiah respectfully asked his king.

"Elijah is to be crowned," Seth breathed. "He may be young, but he is the one next in line to take the throne. He will accompany us in battle to prove himself courageous, worthy to wear the eastern crown. His presence in battle will convince the eastern people of his ability to rule in bravery and confidence. You must ensure his safety, because he is the only one left to take up the crown."

Seth's hand reached over the staff, and he took it back into his grip, his rough and wrinkled skin not feeling the coolness of the gold.

"I will be of as excellent service to him as I am to you, my king," Jeremiah comforted his king as they began to leave the room.

"I know you will be, just as your father was to both Elijah and I," Seth spoke as Jeremiah opened the door for Seth, and they walked into the hallway. "I am going to the sacred garden now, and after I am finished there I will return to you. I will meet you at the city gates. Be prepared with the army."

"Yes, my king," Jeremiah whispered, bowing before the king as they then walked the opposite direction in the hallway.

As Seth began to quickly march down the hallway, Elijah ran up to him from behind, his boots dragging across the red carpet that ran along the center of the hallway.

"Father," Elijah called to Seth as he caught up beside him, "what is happening? The festivities are continuing on, but something is deathly wrong."

"There is no time for explanation," Seth told Elijah. "Prepare yourself for battle. I will come find you once I myself have prepared, and we will join the eastern army in the city."

"I don't understand," Elijah spoke confused at the things his father was telling him, only giving to his son a fraction of what was truly happening.

"You don't need to!" Seth yelled at Elijah, causing Elijah to freeze, as Seth continued down the hall as quick as he could. "There is no time for explanation. Do as I say."

"Jeremiah!" Micah called to his brother amidst the loud group of assembled soldiers that crowded near the gates of the Kingdom of Abel, pushing through the crowd, walking up to the front of the herd of warriors, where Jeremiah stood. "Jeremiah!"

"What is it, Micah?" Jeremiah asked as Micah reached his brother who was standing outside of the group of men, with Seth, Elijah, and the army generals.

Seth took notice of Micah.

"Jeremiah, what is going on?" Micah asked him, everyone still confused as to what was happening.

"You will be informed at the same moment everyone else is," Jeremiah said, gently pushing Micah back into the crowd of warriors. "All I will tell you is that I hope you have practiced with your sword as much you have been with your flute. Your musical skills will do you no good where we are going."

Seth then took a step forward, toward the crowd, and raised his hands, causing complete silence to fall over the entire city that was witnessing this new chapter in history.

"Listen now to what I say!" King Seth announced to the assembled army that filled nearly half of the main roadway that led from the city entrance in the great wall to the entrance of the castle, with many women, older men, and children gathered outside at a distance from the army. "Though this is a day that we remember the fallen prince, by putting away all work and normal daily life, and replacing it with feasts and celebration, I regret that this year's Day of Feast must end prematurely."

Elijah stared at his father from behind where Seth stood, still unaware of what was happening, as Micah stood at twice the distance, from Seth's front side, as part of the front line of warriors dressed in armor like the eastern warriors Seth had led sixteen years ago. Some of the men in the crowd were even apart of the last battle with the west in what was now the great meadow before the fog barrier.

Every eye was on Seth, even Mary's, who was watching from her bedroom balcony, her maidens beside her, but they could not hear anything because of the long distance between them. Seth had informed Mary of everything that was to happen before he told her farewell, and departed the castle.

"The reason we must end it early is the very reason we have it at all." Seth spoke with a sense of strong authority, the crowds gasping at his words as he revealed what was happening in their land. "I fear that the beast, that was released when the oldest of us were children, has returned from the depths of the earth. While we don't know this for sure, we believe that the western queen has been killed, and this beast is roaming freely, like it did those many years ago when Cain set him loose. We, as an army, will march out to the meadow, and await the beast to reveal itself from the fog barrier. From there, we will draw it back to the pit from where it first came, and forcefully return it to the depths. If there is hope in the east, then surely we will prevail in battle against such a horrific beast, and terrible odds."

Elijah, his hands rattling with fear, felt the rugged hair of a white horse as one walked up next to him, pushing against him. Elijah turned to it, seeing that it was one of the Diadem, and he began to pet its side. The Diadem could sense Elijah's worries rising.

"We will leave now, and return once we have ensured the safety of the entire eastern realm," Seth closed his speech, turning toward the Diadem, Elijah, Jeremiah, and the army generals, as the crowd of warriors began to file into many straight lines.

"You will prove yourself worthy of the crown on this journey, my son," Seth said, resting his right hand on Elijah's left shoulder, the weight of fear within Elijah being replaced by the affirmation coming from his father's touch. "You will do so, just as I did, those many years ago."

Battle in the Meadow

The entire army of the Kingdom of Abel lined up in three long rows, running parallel with the fog barrier, stretching out to a tiring distance. All the warriors had a sword sheathed upon their thigh, while the first row also carried spears, the second row carried axes, and the third row in the back carried bows and arrows. In front of the first row were the five generals, evenly spread out across the whole line, with Jeremiah far ahead of the line of generals, sitting on a large grey stallion, his sword already in his hand, ready to fight at a moment's notice, like a tree's roots thirsty for water in the middle of a rainless summer. This whole crowd was a short distance away from the fog barrier, standing in the stillness of the night that had fallen over the land. Faint hues of blue could be spotted coming from the east, as dawn was drawing near.

Behind this brigade of warriors were Seth and Elijah, riding atop the two Diadem, who were in the shape of horses. The opal stones on Seth's crown reflected the white light of the moon, pronouncing defiance against the evil that desired to come into the east once again.

It had been several hours since the army had reached the great meadow, and mobilized into this position to wait for whatever may be coming from the fog barrier that remained as still as the sand it hovered over.

What sounded like a soft thud began to call out from behind the veil of fog at a rhythm that was almost hypnotizing, attempting to strike fear into the hearts of the eastern warriors. With every downbeat, the soft sound of thudding grew into the sound of thousands of footsteps being taken, accompanied by a harmony of clanking metal, the vibrations running up the legs of the eastern warriors, with their feet firmly planted on the meadow ground they stood on.

Jeremiah silently raised his sword into the air, causing every member of the army to draw their weapons, including Elijah who pulled out his sword. Seth sat calmly upon his Diadem, waiting to see what was about to happen, not exactly sure what to expect.

A faint drop of sweat rolled down the side of Micah's face that was hidden beneath the heavy silver helmet, as he gripped his sword tightly, with his bow and quiver hanging from his back.

The sound suddenly became twice as fast, and the sound of metal clanking was completely overcome by the sound of something slamming against the ground within the fog. The earth beneath the eastern army's feet began to tremble as they stared at the fog barrier, Jeremiah at their lead ready to command them into battle.

Suddenly, a vulture drenched in black feathers shot out from the fog barrier, high above the crowd, catching the attention of all the men of the east. Silently, this vulture with ruby colored eyes circled over the army, as the nostrils of the eastern Diadem flared up, puffs of steam shooting out in anger against their fallen brother who was flying over them.

Following this, came Oliver riding on the back of the other western Diadem that was in the form of an oversized wolf, its fur blacker than the darkest raincloud. Oliver, dressed in black armor with a short silver cape hanging from the back of his shoulders, slowly rode out toward Jeremiah.

"She must be dead," Elijah whispered to his father, the two of them intently watching Oliver. "I can't imagine a Diadem would ever leave someone of royalty alone in such a time of battle."

Seth seemingly ignored his son, giving no response, and kept his complete focus on what was happening as the Diadem high above continued flying in circles.

"This is unexpected," Oliver called out to Jeremiah, as he, on the Diadem he rode, came to a stop about ten feet in front of Jeremiah, who remained unshaken in this time of uncertainty. "The last time our western fathers fought on these grounds, your eastern fathers were not so punctual."

"And this land was much less void," Oliver added, looking around at the open meadow that the eastern army stood in.

"Whatever it is you have come here to do," Jeremiah boldly interrupted Oliver, "you will not succeed."

"No force you hold can contain us to the west any longer," Oliver responded, turning back toward the fog barrier, and just as slowly trotted back into the fog, with the Diadem as a vulture returning into the fog as well.

Complete silence returned to the meadow as the eastern army awaited the commands of Jeremiah, the dark blue eastern sky warming to lighter shades as the morning became anxious to reveal itself, and watch the battle that was about to begin.

A single deep blast of a ram's horn suddenly exploded from within the fog barrier, and shortly following this sound came a wave of western warriors draped in the same type of metal armor that their father's wore, bursting out from the fog, running out toward the eastern army. They were unorganized, running in a sloppy row out from the fog, and were numerically only about as many as the eastern army had in its first row.

Immediately, Jeremiah spun his sword in the air over his head, the signal for the army to run up before him and the generals, to meet the enemy in battle.

Sword struck sword, and sword struck shield; sword struck

armor, and sword pierced skin as the battle began. A second call of the ram's horn belted out from the fog, causing another wave of the western military to fan out from the fog.

"Now, Elijah!" Seth yelled at his son, and with that, Elijah slid off of the Diadem, and ran into battle, his sword gripped tightly in his hand, his fears being shutdown by the greater hope and courage that dwelled in the depths of his heart.

Seth's eyes darted about the fight as his son disappeared amongst the fighting that ensued as a third blast sounded out from the fog, the tree lining behind the meadow toward the east becoming clearly visible in the sky that was waiting for the dawn to awake.

Micah's sword slashed away at the western enemies that came his way, though his shield took more hits than his sword gave, while Elijah bolted around the battleground, slicing at the ankles of the enemy forces as he did, causing many to collapse.

A large western warrior jumped out toward Elijah, swinging his sword at Elijah's head. Elijah rose his shield and sword up, but the enemy struck Elijah's sword violently with his own, causing it to fly from Elijah's grip. The enemy then kicked at Elijah's shield with great force, causing Elijah to fall backward onto the ground.

The enemy ran up to Elijah, and looked down at the prince. Standing over Elijah, who had covered his body with his shield, the enemy threw his own shield down, grabbed his sword handle with both hands, his grip as tight as he could make it, lifted his sword high above his own head, and prepared to slice it down at Elijah's shield, expecting to break through its thin metal, and pierce Elijah in the chest.

From where Jeremiah rode his horse, a short distance away, he saw Elijah lying defenseless against this western warrior, and began charging toward their direction, slamming his ankles into his stallion's side, forcing it to bolt through the crowd of fighting.

With less than a breath's time before the enemy thrust down his sword at Elijah, an arrow shot into his arm, penetrating his armor. Then, a second into one of his hands, and then a third penetrating his breast plate, lodging itself into his heart, all the arrows shot within two seconds. The enemy fell backward onto the ground, leaving Elijah alive.

"Hurry!" Micah's voice sounded from behind as he ran up to Elijah, with his bow in his left hand.

Stretching his open right hand to the prince, Elijah grabbed on, and pulled himself up onto his feet again while the fight continued around them.

"Thank you," Elijah told Micah, his eyes hooked on Micah's eyes for a brief moment, interrupted by Jeremiah arriving on his stallion.

"There is no time for discussion!" Jeremiah yelled amidst the chaos around the three of them.

With that, the two quickly went back into battle, Elijah grabbing his sword back from the ground as he ran off, ready to carry on with fighting, encouraged to see that his fellow eastern brothers were watchful of him and his safety.

The eastern army was easily overcoming the western army as Seth continued to watch from his seat on the Diadem. His eyes had gone from watching over his son, to searching for Oliver.

"Something is not right," Seth softly spoke aloud to his Diadem, and with that, a fourth blast came from the fog, but this time, it was a higher pitched call.

Every remaining member of the western army suddenly bolted back into the fog, escaping the losing fight they had fallen into, with the sky in the east still lightening up as dawn neared, but the sun was still nowhere to be found.

Cheering came from the eastern army because they assumed that this was the end of the battle. Jeremiah looked toward his king, to see him unmoved. With this, Jeremiah rapidly called the entire army back into their rows, and Elijah, caught up in the excitement of this battle, did not return to his father's side, but, instead, got into the first row of men, standing near the center.

Once again, silence fell over the darkened meadow, but it was choked out by the sound of birds chirping in the distant surrounding forests, and eerie stillness fell over the area, with the bodies of fallen warriors scattered across the meadow where the eastern army had reassembled.

Seth, upon his Diadem, then trotted out, passing through the rows of warriors, looking for Elijah. As this happened, Oliver reappeared from the fog barrier without Seth noticing, and Oliver, still on the Diadem's back, rode out up to Jeremiah.

"This is a warning," Oliver spoke out to Jeremiah as he paused ten feet away from him. "Surrender now or we will attack again, and fight until your army has completely fallen."

"It is obvious we were winning in battle," Jeremiah responded to Oliver, still breathing heavily as his adrenalin rushed within his body. "It is the west who should surrender."

"Where is Elijah?" Seth called out loudly as he searched through the gathered warriors, his worried voice traveling to where Oliver and Jeremiah stood. "Where is he?"

"Your king seems to have lost one of his favorite warriors," Oliver mocked, amused by Seth wandering around upon his Diadem.

"Where are you, Elijah?" Seth yelled, with Elijah breaking formation in line, and turning to Seth, visible to Oliver who was facing this direction.

"Here I am, father!" Elijah excitedly yelled out to Seth, Seth's eyes quickly finding his son.

"Father?!" Oliver yelled out, in confusion and shock. "An

heir to the eastern throne lives?!"

Within the blink of an eye, Oliver and his Diadem spun around, and raced back into the fog barrier, with the speed and force of rain drops falling in the harshest of showers, in the lowest of valleys.

The second eastern Diadem quickly went up to Elijah, still in the form of a white horse, and Elijah jumped upon his back. Without warning, the incredible stomping that had sounded from the fog continued again, and the earth shook violently, tossing some of the warriors off of their feet, and onto the ground.

Before anyone could realize what was happening, Plague burst out of the fog barrier, with Olivia riding upon the top of his head, her hands firmly grasping onto his scales for security. The air became thin with the many warriors gasping as they saw this. Plague came to a stop twenty-five feet away from Jeremiah, and fear pierced into the hearts of everyone from the east at the sight of this wretched beast, and the beautiful queen that rode on him.

"Where is he?!" Olivia roared out as the warriors who had just collapsed all got back up to their feet, weapons all across the army raised high.

Olivia quickly saw Elijah sitting upon one of the Diadem, her father on the other Diadem at his side, as the sky in the east became warm with the sunrays that were about to shoot forth from behind the forest at any moment, breaking the darkness of these moments before dawn.

"A prince in the east?!" Olivia screamed, slapping her hands against the rough scales of Plague's head, directing him to run at Elijah.

The same violent pounding vibrated again as Plague ran across the ground, his feet stomping as he raced at Elijah, dirt and grass being torn and tossed into the air behind him.

Jeremiah tried to get in Plague's way, but Plague swatted at him with his head, causing him and his stallion to be thrown backward through the air, crashing into the front row of warriors.

"Jeremiah!" Micah screamed as he, and three of his nearby brothers, ran to Jeremiah.

Being about thirty feet away from Elijah, Plague pounced into the air, ready to land in front of Elijah, and swallow him up. Before Plague landed, the sun was suddenly revealed, shooting its rays of light like cannons at Plague, causing him to thrash backward in midair, with Olivia falling off of his head, and onto the ground.

Horrible screeching sounded from Plague as his thrashing body painfully flopped around in the sunlight. Moving away from the army, he quickly found his way back into the fog, and sunk back into its shadows, away from the light.

"Your beast has failed you," Seth said to Olivia as he quickly rode up to her, where she was lying on her back on the ground. "No beast of darkness, no matter how powerful, can stand in the light."

"You're a fool for thinking you can stop me," Olivia growled at her father, getting back onto her feet, as she stood alone before the entire eastern army, her eyes then quickly shifting back to Elijah. "You're an even greater fool to think that you could crown a new king in the east without me interfering."

"You could not overcome the Kingdom of Abel sixteen years ago," Seth spoke down to his daughter from his seat on the Diadem, her eyes returning to Seth, "and you cannot overcome the Kingdom of Abel this day."

"Like you told me, all those years ago, father," Olivia responded as one of her Diadem raced out from the fog barrier as an oversized hyena, hurrying to the western queen's side, "I did what I came to do. We now stand in the clearing that was once home to the people I came to destroy. The only hope the east had against me came from that village, but it, along with all its entire population, went up in flames. Your persistence, when it comes to survival, confuses me."

Elijah gripped tightly onto his sword as Olivia turned her gaze back on him where he remained away from her. A sense of awareness built up over her as realization struck her thoughts, causing her greatest fears to blossom.

"It can't be." Olivia's voice shook as the Diadem scooped her between her legs, placing the queen on his back. "It can't be. There could not be a survivor from that day."

Elijah threw down his shield, and with that hand took off his helmet to reveal his face to Olivia. His lighter than average skin almost shined in the light, the dark aqua of his damp and sweaty hair easily visible with the lighting of the sun revealing more than just his appearance. In this moment of fighting, Elijah's fears seemed to have vanished, overtaken by immeasurable courage he had found within him to defy evil.

"You bear no resemblance to our family, and your skin is much paler than anyone from the eastern city," Olivia said, her eyes as wide as they could go, fear overflowing from her heart. "This cannot be."

"Return to the darkness, Olivia!" Seth ordered his cowering daughter, whose eyes could not separate from Elijah. "Go back to the west."

"Do you think that you have won?" Olivia turned her attention back on her father. "Just as the sun has risen, the sun will set, again. Know that when it does, just as my army has left, it will return."

"Then we will await your return," Seth said as the hyena began to take steps backward, away from Seth.

"Your army may be waiting," Olivia slyly spoke, reaching her hand into her boot, hiding this action by seemingly gripping onto the

Diadem's side "but you won't be, father!"

From her boot, Olivia pulled out a dagger, and threw it at her father as she and her Diadem raced back into the fog even faster than Oliver had just done. Upon impact with Seth, the force of the dagger threw Seth off the Diadem.

"Father!" Elijah yelled, fear refilling into his heart as he jumped off his Diadem, ran to the king on the ground, and kneeled beside Seth.

Seth looked to Elijah as the silver dagger that had sunk into his shoulder began to spill out blood beneath the royal robes.

"I am fine Elijah," Seth said as Elijah grabbed onto his father's hands, "do not fear."

The five generals quickly surrounded the two royals.

"My king," one of the generals said urgently, "we must get you back to the Kingdom of Abel at once. Your injury cannot be tended to here. Though she threw this dagger with poor aim, it has not struck you lightly."

"The Diadem will return Elijah and I back to the kingdom," Seth spoke softly, the pain of the injury swelling within him. "You must all stay here, in case the western army returns. If they don't by noontime tomorrow, send half of our warriors back to the kingdom, and leave behind watchmen to return to the kingdom with warning if an attack is to come."

"My king!" Jeremiah spoke out, stumbling toward Seth, falling about five feet away from where Seth was lying down, barely conscious from the hit when Plague knocked him down.

"Jeremiah, you must rest!" Micah called to Jeremiah, catching up to his brother on the ground. "You will be fine, but you must at least sit for a moment."

"Thank you for your concern over my health," Seth said to his loyal followers as Jeremiah tried sitting up, "but tend to Jeremiah, and the other ones injured here. I will be fine."

"But the queen warned us that she would return," one of the generals said to Seth confused. "She has revealed her plan to us."

Seth turned from his generals, and back to Elijah.

"Let us go now," Seth muttered, causing the two Diadem to prepare to transform into creatures that could safely fly the two back to the palace.

Seth lay down in his large bed, beneath heavy white wool sheets, on the bed's edge, as Elijah, Mary, and Benjamin, an elder who served as one of King Seth's most trusted advisors, stood at his bedside. Much of the color in his skin had left his face, and he was hardly conscious, only awake from the pain that filled his tired body. Though the dagger had not struck any organs, a mix of his age and loss of blood resulted in this life threatening moment. The weapon had been removed from his shoulder, and the wound was wrapped in a thick tourniquet that kept the bleeding down to a minimum. Though he was not dressed in royal attire, the crown remained on his head.

"This is only a taste of the bitter times that are to follow us here," Benjamin said, standing upright, wearing long brown robes of fine fabric.

"Is there nothing we can do?" Mary asked, nearly hopeless.

"For our king?" Benjamin asked back to Mary as Elijah stood silent by his father whose eyelids were opening and closing as he wheezed for breath.

"For any of us," Mary responded as Seth slowly turned his face to his son who was standing closest to his head, though he did not interrupt his wife. "It's nearly noontime. Once the sun sets, the only real defense we have against the beast will be the distance from the meadow to our kingdom."

"The distance is too great for the western army to reach our kingdom and retreat back to the west in one night," Benjamin responded. "Being trapped in the east when the sun rises is too great a risk for the beast to take. He, and his rebel brethren, have dwelled in the dark for such a length of time that they can no longer stand the light of day. The western military won't be stopped by the sunlight, only slowed down for a short while until their eyesight can adjust to the brightness. Most of them have never even seen the light of day before."

"Olivia is unpredictable," Mary added. "Who knows what she will do, especially now that she knows of Elijah."

"Elijah…" Seth whispered to his son, causing Benjamin and Mary to cease their talking. "I need you to get me a drink."

"Yes," Elijah said, quickly turning and reaching for a bronze cup that was on a small chest beside the king's bed.

"No," Seth softly breathed, Elijah turning back to him, "not that. Take an empty glass, and go to the sacred garden. Bring me back a glass of the water that's in there for me to drink. Go."

"But, my king," Benjamin spoke out, "nobody except the one who wears the crown that is on your head has ever entered there."

"Go," Seth repeated, outright ignoring Benjamin, a sight never seen before.

At this, Elijah turned away, and rushed out of the room.

Mary sat on the edge of the bed, and placed her hand onto her husband's forehead, bringing warmth to his cold skin, as his eyes slowly fell closed.

"I will leave you," Benjamin told Mary as he respectfully walked out of the room, shutting the door behind him, joining Mary's five maidens in the hallway.

"Oh, Seth," Mary softly said as she sat beside her dying husband.

The worry in her soul began to combat against the hope she had always depended on as her fingertips grazed the thin strands of white hair on his head. She placed her other hand on his folded hands that rested on top of his stomach, Seth's hands hidden beneath the bed sheets.

As softly as she could, she began to sing the eastern song of hope over him, hoping to sooth away the pain with her gentle voice, while tears slowly dripped down her face, soaking into the soft pillow Seth's head rested on. His breathing seemed to slow down to a regular pace as she continued to quietly sing.

The Sacred Garden

Elijah stared at the tall silver doors that were the entrance to the sacred garden, his reflection slightly visible on the mirror-like doors. The only men who had ever seen the garden on the other side of these doors were the kings of the east, during their reign. Not even the queens, princes who were not heirs to the throne, or princesses, had ever gazed into it, and the details of it had never been shared to others before. It was seen as an inheritance received by the newly crowned eastern kings.

An empty glass Elijah had obtained on his walk to this place was in his left hand, and with his right, he reached out to a door handle, pulling it toward him, opening the door. Elijah, tilting his head down to look at the brick laid ground of the castle roof beneath his feet, speedily slid into the garden, quickly letting the door shut behind him, leaving him in the solitude of the enclosed room.

All over his body he felt a reverence that he had never before felt, almost causing the hair on the back of his neck to rise, like the arms of a child reaching out to its father. He was in the presence of someone greater than any king that reigned on the entire earth before, both in the Kingdoms of Abel, Cain, and uncharted lands. Beneath his heavy brown boots was growing dark green grass that only grew a couple inches tall. Fearful of trampling over the lush grass beneath him with his rough boots, Elijah unbuckled his boots, and made himself barefoot, the grass feeling like the softest cotton against his calloused feet. Mustering up the courage that hid deep within him, he slowly raised his head up, facing the inside of the silver doorway he had just walked through, once again seeing an outline of his reflection in the silver. His breaths became short and silent as he slowly turned around, and in awe, took in the sight of the room.

The entire floor of the room was covered in soft grass, and the marble walls were so clean they almost appeared to be mirrors. The lighting of the room was very dim, with soft white lights glowing from the flower buds that were facing down from the lowest branches of an olive tree that was growing in the center of the room. At the foot of the tree was a small pond that reflected the light from the flowers. The small lights were also reflecting off of the walls, making it as though Elijah was caught up in the night sky, stars burning calmly from a distance all around. There was complete tranquility in this place that seemed to be frozen still. This place was the most beautiful thing Elijah had ever laid his eyes on or experienced.

Slowly taking steps, moving toward the center of the room, Elijah looked up to the branches to see two small white eagles perched in the branches looking down at him; they were the Diadem.

Once Elijah reached the tree, he gently rubbed his hand against the bark, and a sudden burst of energy and life began to fill his veins. The wood was extremely smooth, like no other tree in the forests surrounding the kingdom. He looked up to its branches, trying to see past the countless number of leaves, but was unable to because of the density of the branches. He recognized the flowers of the tree to resemble the flowers that were upon his father's crown. Though the room looked like it should be cold, Elijah could feel a sense of warmth all over his body that brought comfort and hope to his worried soul.

Recalling his reason for coming to this room, and the urgency of the matter, he turned his head down to the small pond at his feet. Kneeling down at the still body of water, he tenderly swooped the glass in his hand across the pond's surface, collecting its water into his glass, stirring up ripples that danced and motioned over the water, distorting the reflection of himself Elijah had first seen when looking into the water.

Elijah's attention was grabbed by the pond's surface as he saw his reflection begin to change in the rippling of the water. The reflection showed his rugged brown tunic falling off of his body, and beneath the tunic were linen green robes that were fit for a king, with a necklace of brilliant red-orange bird feathers sprinkled with splashed black speckles across them, hanging from his neck, covering over his chest. The youthful skin on his face became covered by trimmed black facial hair, and the hair on his head was slicked back, holding up the crown that the kings of the east had always worn. As the ripples intensified, this image in the pond became clearer to Elijah, but as the ripples began to fade away, so did this image of foresight. Stillness fell back upon the water's surface, and Elijah saw himself as he currently was.

Elijah was left completely speechless, unsure if he had even actually seen something, or if his mind were playing tricks on him in this place that was unlike any other place he had been in. He tried to convince himself that his imagination had tried to rob his eyes of clear sight for a moment, taking advantage of the motioning water he had peered into.

Holding the glass tightly against his chest, he rose back up onto his feet, and turned away from the pond, walking toward the exit where his boots were waiting to be used again.

"Father," Elijah whispered to Seth who was in a slumber, though the sun was only now beginning to set over the castle, as the two were alone in the room. "Father, wake up."

Seth slowly began to wake, though he was very groggy, holding onto life with the weakest of grips. His eyelids, hardly opened up at all, fought against his eyes for sight as his face turned to Elijah who stood at his bedside, a cup in his hand filled with the water from the sacred garden.

"I have brought you the drink you requested," Elijah gently said, putting the cup to Seth's now violet lips, slightly tilting the glass, pouring the water into his mouth.

At first, the gulps Seth took were extremely slow, but with each gulp his swallowing became faster, and he seemed to be gaining energy back into his body immediately. Veins that had become evident across his exposed skin began to sink back into him as his skin tone returned to its normal color. His eyes began to squint, and then his eyes were opened fully as he took the last couple sips of the water. The coldness that had fallen over his whole body began to shatter as heat within him pushed the chill away.

Elijah, lowering the glass from his lips that were back to a healthy red, set the empty glass on the table by the bed as Seth used his own renewed strength to sit up. Reaching for the tourniquet over his shoulder, he unwrapped it to find that the wound that was hidden by the cloth was miraculously gone.

"Your obedience has saved me," Seth said clearly, turning back to Elijah, Seth's body back to full health. "The water from the sacred garden has healed me."

"I will go get mother," Elijah responded, Seth grabbing onto his shoulder with a youthful strength.

"Wait," Seth stopped Elijah from turning away. "Before you go, know this, Elijah. You have done something that no other person has done before. The sacred garden was meant for kings, and kings alone. But, because you have entered in, and brought me this water that returned health to my dying body, you may enter into the garden again as you please, but take no other person with you, ever."

"Thank you, my king," Elijah said as Seth sat further up in bed, and turned his body to the bed's side, his feet dangling off its edge, ready to walk away from his bed.

"Now, let us get back to the task at hand," Seth said, standing up, with Elijah rushing to get Seth's royal robes that were laid out on the other end of his bed. "There is still a war to be won."

"We cannot risk your safety again, my king," Jeremiah spoke as he sat at a large table with Seth, Elijah, Benjamin, the five generals, and several other of Seth's advisors. "We must change our course of action."

"Whether I am put in harm's way, or not, there is no other person left to remove the onyx seal," Seth argued. "Olivia is the only other one with royal blood, and she would only remove the seal once more if she were to free additional beasts, not return this one back. There is no other person."

"We've almost lost you once," Benjamin interjected. "We

cannot run the chance of your health wavering again. Yes, there is an heir if something is to happen, and you are to fall, but our goal is not to have an heir to replace you; it is your safety."

"If my life must be lost so that countless others would not be, then so be it," Seth boldly stated, causing Elijah to push his chair away from the table, stand up, and rush out of the room.

This was the first thing Elijah had done in the meeting that had already been going on since earlier that evening.

"I will not put my own life before my kingdom's," Seth breathed out as the door behind Elijah closed, and the men in the room lowered their heads in sorrow. "We all have our time to leave this life, and if this is my time, so be it."

"There must be another way," one of the five generals continued on, the men not satisfied with Seth's willingness to end his reign.

"Surely, there must be a way to get you to the pit safely, without being seen," another general added.

"Yes," Jeremiah fueled the flame of hope for Seth's survival, "There must be a way."

Elijah again found himself standing at the entrance to the sacred garden, hidden in the night's shadows atop the castle. After taking off his boots, he pulled open the doorway, and walked back into the sacred garden, the same stunning awe overtaking him as the silver door behind him closed.

Sitting at the foot of a white marble bench on one end of the garden was one of the Diadem in the form of a white tiger with silver stripes, stoically seated as Elijah took his first few steps into the room.

"My father is planning to return to the war," Elijah told the tiger, beginning to walk in its direction. "You must go and protect him."

With that, the second Diadem, in the form of a small white dove, swooped down from within the crowded tree branches, carrying a small branch in its beak. The thin branch had a few leaves on it, and three small closed flower buds.

Landing on Elijah's shoulder, Elijah's eyes turned from the tiger to the dove, noticing the branch in its beak.

Cautiously, Elijah reached his hand to the Diadem's beak, and carefully took the branch from its mouth, and into his hand, holding it with his fingertips. Instantly, the closed flower buds began to blossom, and beautiful flowers in bloom dominated over the weak piece of branch it was attached to.

Elijah's eyes marveled at the sight of the morphed flowers, and with that, the dove retreated back into the branches of the tree, near the bark.

"Wait!" Elijah said, running toward where the dove flew into the tree, quickly reaching the smooth tree bark. "What does this mean? How will this help my father?"

Elijah's arms wrapped around the tree, and with the leather wrapped around his hands, began to grip onto the bark, pulling himself up, using his bare feet to help push him up as well. As he pulled himself up the bark, and reached the bottom branches, his hands latched onto the branches, and he lifted himself up above the low-lying branches.

Getting solid footing on the branches that were now below him, he looked to the dove, which was perched on a branch about two feet above his head, near the center bark that continued to grow upward, all the branches extending outward from it.

Climbing up a little bit more, he became eye level with the dove that was covered in white feathers which were radiating the dim light that shined from the flowers beneath it. Elijah's attention then went from the dove, to a parcel wrapped in brown leather that was wedged between the branch the dove was resting on, and the thick center bark.

Taking the parcel into his hands, the dove dived down into the air, and flew out from the tree.

Elijah's hands, his fingertips feeling the smoothness of the leather object he had found, began to unwrap the parcel that was tied together with a piece of golden rope. Removing the rope and leather wrapping, Elijah found a small journal with a faded red covering.

Opening it, Elijah skimmed across the thick pages of aged paper, finding hundreds of pages littered with words and sketches of all sorts of things etched in black ink. Between two pages, Elijah found a brilliant red-orange feather with black spots sprinkled over it, and on one of the pages where this feather had been found were sketches of birds that were dressed in feathers like the one the book held. In comparison to the pages of the journal, this feather placed in it did not seem to be aged at all. On the other page that was touching this feather was a paragraph detailing the peculiar habits of this bird, including their ability to sing beautiful songs, and how they fed off of large bushels of fruit from the trees they lived in. Beneath this paragraph was a map to where they were solely found, in a part of the forest that was days away from the eastern kingdom, in a place where Elijah recognized to now be the meadow.

Without warning, the dove landed back on Elijah's shoulder, again carrying in its beak the small branch it had first given to Elijah, who, in the rush of catching up to the Diadem that flew into the tree, had dropped the blossomed branch.

"Is this what you wanted me to find?" Elijah questioned, beginning to flip through the pages, when suddenly, the Diadem dropped the branch into the flapping pages, turning the branch into a bookmark.

Noticing this, Elijah turned back to the pages that the branch had fallen between, and found fantastic sketches of armor, with descriptions of each of the six parts of the outfit. The uniform consisted of a belt, boots, a breastplate, a shield, a helmet, and a sword. The designs of each of these was unlike anything Elijah had ever seen, and as he looked over the next few pages, reading the text that went along with the drawings, found maps that led to each of the pieces of the armor that seemed to be scattered in places Elijah had never seen or heard of, far away from the east or west that he knew.

Elijah closed the book, and the Diadem that was nestled on his shoulder took flight, returning back beneath the tree. With that, Elijah began to climb down the tree, prepared to return to the meeting he had just walked out on. On his way down the tree, he looked back up toward the top of the tree that was still hidden due to the density of branches and leaves. Curiosity stirred within Elijah, but he knew he would have to wait to explore the rest of this tree another time.

A Way

"If there is then no other way…" Benjamin said at the table, those in attendance coming to terms with the impending doom of their king, but his sentence was suddenly interrupted by the doors to the meeting room swinging open, with Elijah running in.

"There is another way!" Elijah boldly said, quickly walking up to his father who sat in the largest chair at the table, the book from the sacred garden in Elijah's hands. "The royal armor."

"My boy," one of the advisors responded as Elijah walked to his father. "Obtaining those six pieces would take years, and the location of them was lost with the passing of the first king. Even we in here do not have enough hope for that."

"Then may this give you hope," Elijah replied, reaching Seth's side, handing to him the journal of the first king.

Opening it, Seth's eyes became stunned as he looked through

its pages, quickly landing on the page bookmarked by the blossomed branch, where the information about the royal armor was recorded.

"My eyes can barely believe what they see." Seth breathed heavily, turning his face back toward his son. "Where did you find this?"

"It was in the sacred garden," Elijah explained, "hidden in the branches of the tree."

Seth looked back down to the book, then back up to those sitting at the table, and then said, "I wish to privately meet with Benjamin, Jeremiah, and Elijah."

The others that were sitting at the table then stood up, and walked out of the meeting room, the doors shutting behind them as they obediently left.

"This is the journal of the first king of the east," Seth explained to the last three men in the room. "Answers to many secrets of this land are within the pages of this book, including the location of the armor that can slay the beasts that were trapped beneath the earth, one of which is the very enemy we are facing now."

"My king," Benjamin said, "even with the knowledge of their location, there is still no time to retrieve all the pieces before Olivia figures out a way for the beast to reach us here."

"How do you know that?" Seth debated. "How do we know

that the beast can ever reach us here? Perhaps we are always safe from it reaching us."

"Would you jeopardize the safety of this kingdom over a theory?" Benjamin challenged the king in a submissive tone.

"Not over a theory," Seth remarked, "but I would over hopeful chance, and I believe there is always hope."

"What then will you have us do, my king?" Jeremiah asked Seth.

"I must study the details of this journal more," Seth answered, closing the book, and setting it on his lap. "Return to your homes, and in two evenings from now, we will continue this meeting."

Seth sat alone in the meeting room, several candles burning on the table he sat at, reading the pages of the journal that brought many secrets and wonders to light. The information this journal contained was bringing many answers to questions that had formed over the generations since the first king.

Seth read about the onyx seals, learning things he did not know about them being opened, including how the beasts could call forth darkness to fall over the land that they were released in, so they could travel through it safely, away from the light of day. The heavy blanket of darkness over the west was contained to the west because the seal in the west had been opened. Were the seal in the east to be opened, the same fate could potentially fall upon the east. The only way the curse of darkness could be lifted was if the beast that caused it were to be slain.

Reading on, he learned of the six pieces of the armor that could slay the beasts beneath the earth, and which lands the six pieces had been hidden in throughout the unknown world. A map of the world was sketched in the journal as well, leaving Seth with an image so foreign to him that he could not truly understand it. Seth could hardly comprehend the idea that there were more than the two realms of the Kingdoms of Abel and Cain. The author of this journal, the first king, had not been to these places, but had somehow seen them with his own eyes, though even the secret of how this was done was not in the writings of this journal.

Following this section, Seth skipped to the area where the feather was left as a bookmark. His eyes became fixated on the drawings of the unique animals that were sketched into the pages. He could recall hearing of these animals, as though they were myths, passed on to the people in the city from interaction with the people from the forest village. He could remember, as a small child, hearing the stories of beautiful birds of bright colors, with designs never seen on any other animal, and deer that were shades of the sky at dawn with fantastic antlers that were like leafless branches. There were several other animals he remembered hearing of as a child, that he now saw sketches of, along with recorded details of their behaviors, in this journal.

The journal told of the first king coming to a part of the forest, where these animals were in abundance. At this location were also trees that stood taller than any other trees around, and produced massive bushels of fruit. Seth continued studying to find out why the king had come to this place.

"The sun has set twice since I have begun this walk away from the kingdom we have finally finished constructing," Seth silently read. *"The voice from the sky has led me here, to this place in the forest, further from my people than anyone of us have ever gone. He has brought me to this place to bury the crown first given to me, so that I, and kings after me, may wear a crown of gold and opal. Along with where to bury this crown, the One also told me why I was to bury it here..."*

Astonished by the following portion of text he read, Seth shut the book, and stared at its timeless cover. What he had just read left him in complete shock.

Realization at how this very book could become a weapon in the hands of the one holding it, using its secrets as an advantage in war, began to overcome Seth. He realized the greater danger that could come over his kingdom if the enemy were to learn of this journal in his possession.

Over the next two days, half the eastern military had returned to the Kingdom of Abel, as Seth had ordered for them to do if the western army did not show themselves. Among the returning soldiers was Micah, who was eager to reunite with his older brother, Jeremiah. The other half of the military were left in the meadow, with renewed orders from their king to wait seven more days, and after then, return to the kingdom, leaving behind a handful of watchmen. If the western army still did not show themselves, certain warriors would be selected to be sent out on rotation to be watchmen in the wide meadow, awaiting any signs of the Kingdom of Cain.

"What is to happen now, Jeremiah?" Micah asked his brother as he took a seat at the table Jeremiah sat at, in the first room of the small house they had grown up in. "Are we to wait another several years for Olivia to return?"

Jeremiah sat silent, completely unresponsive to his brother's questions, Jeremiah's eyes staring at the smooth wooden table that held clean cups and plates at each empty chair. In several hours, he would be back in the meeting room, with King Seth, to be given orders over the next plan of action in dealing with the war.

"Surely you can say something," Micah complained, wanting to know the plans for the fight ahead.

"Silence, Micah," Jeremiah barked shortly at his brother, turning his head up to face Micah's, Jeremiah slamming his open hand down onto the table, causing the ceramic cups and plates to rattle. "What was spoken in secret will remain in secret."

The two brothers became quiet, alone in the house, and Micah then looked to the tabletop.

"I just want to help," Micah weakly said, intimidated by his older brother.

Silence returned between the two of them for a moment, but the silence was interrupted by the sound of Jeremiah backing his chair away from the table, and Jeremiah's feet dragging along the floor as he walked out of the room, leaving Micah alone in the room, lit by the sunlight coming in through the skylights in their ceiling.

Night soon fell over the Kingdom of Abel, and the meeting between Seth, Benjamin, Jeremiah, and Elijah took place as planned.

"If opening the seal in the eastern lake will bring shadow upon this land," Jeremiah began to plot, filled with much of the new information Seth had received from the journal, and shared with those in this exclusive meeting, "then we must post soldiers to guard that area from the western queen if she attempts to open that seal."

"And what about this journal?" Benjamin debated.

"We must keep it completely hidden," Seth added. "Not just the fact that we have it, but its physical location as well."

"I will return it to where I found it," Elijah offered.

"No," Seth responded, "it must get away from this kingdom.

130

We cannot put the kingdom in danger by means of the enemy taking it from us if they are to hear about its discovery."

"How would they know of its existence at all?" Elijah asked his king.

"The enemy comes in many forms," Seth wisely explained to his son, the others around partaking of the wisdom being shared. "We cannot always know if we are being watched or not. In days of war, great caution must be taken at all times."

"Do you think any of us could be the enemy?" Elijah asked his father, Seth then looking at the other three men in the room dead in the eye, one at a time, with a deafening pause following.

"No," Seth answered, "I do not believe any man at this table would betray the east. Each one would gladly give his life to protect the east. And were any of you given an opportunity to make an agreement with Olivia, handing over our secrets in exchange for your life to be spared, I know that you would rather, without contemplation, die an honorable death of a free man, than become a well fed slave under western ruling."

Another pause followed as the trust this king had in his men was put on display, affirming their loyalty.

"What are we to do then with this knowledge of the onyx seal, and the royal armor?" Jeremiah respectfully asked the king, returning back to what he felt was most important.

"To be cautious, we will send two spies to hide out at the eastern lake," Seth began to command, his followers eager to hear what he had to say. "They are to be well hidden, so to not draw any attention to themselves, or the lake. If anything suspicious is seen, one is to return at once, and the other is to continue watching what he sees. If need be, he will interfere with what is happening. As for the armor, that is a much greater task."

"Whatever you ask of us," Benjamin faithfully said to his king, "we will do it."

"The six pieces of armor are scattered across the unknown lands that surround us," Seth explained, pulling out the journal, and opening it up to pages that were still book marked by the blossomed branch Elijah had received in the garden.

The other men looked to the pages that had sketches of large bodies of lands atop many seas. The idea of seas was foreign to these land dwellers who had never gone to the shores that were far past the surrounding forests around them, seeming to be at least several days away from the ends of the forest they, and none before them, had ever ventured to.

"There are greater bodies of water than any river or lake we have ever seen," Seth attempted to explain. "These bodies of water split one land from another, and they must somehow be crossed so that the hidden pieces of armor can be reached, and obtained. This journal has maps of the locations of all the pieces."

"Are there other people on these foreign lands?" Benjamin questioned.

"I would assume so," Seth answered back, wondering the very same thing in his own mind.

"Send me," Elijah said, his father's eyes striking into Elijah's at these words, "I'll go."

"I will accompany him," Jeremiah bravely added. "I will see that no harm falls upon him."

With Seth's eyes still on his son's, he slowly shut the journal, resting his hands on the closed cover. The unpredictable bravery in his son's heart began to give him a hope for these dark days that had fallen on the east. Amidst the days of war, there was a peace in this king's heart.

"Though I cannot wear the armor myself," Elijah continued to convince his father of his wholehearted bravery, "I will bring you these six pieces to wear, so you can vanquish the rebel beast, and put a stop to the west's war against our people for good."

"My son," Seth began to say to Elijah, "though you were born of another bloodline, I feel as though the same courage that runs in my veins runs in yours. You will go search out these six pieces, and return them to me. Jeremiah, you will accompany him, guarding him with your own life, protecting this heir to the eastern throne."

"And the journal?" Benjamin asked Seth.

"Elijah will take it with him," Seth responded, pushing the book across the table, toward his son, where Elijah reached out for it and took it into his own possession. "Just as Jeremiah guards you, you are to guard the journal. Let nobody know of it, and keep it secret. You can use its pages to guide you to the pieces of armor. Once you have obtained the entire suit, return to the east at once."

"The different locations of the six pieces of armor are so distant from here, and from each other," Elijah said, realizing the magnitude of the journey ahead. "We will be gone for at least a year."

"Yes," Seth responded. "It will be the cost of having the ability to slay the beast."

"What if they are to attack while we are away?" Jeremiah quickly asked. "Or if they figure out a way to reach the Kingdom of Abel with the beast?"

"If we run out of time before your return," Seth answered, "then we will be forced to return to our original plan, and attempt to trap the beast in the pit as I did when I was a child."

"Then let us leave now so that time will be in our favor," Jeremiah said, standing up, ready to begin the journey. "We will take two of the healthiest horses, a small bag of food for each of us, supplies, weapons, and depart at once."

Seth looked back to his son, almost unprepared to let him

leave, and in the most loving of ways said, "Very well."

"Farewell, my son," Mary spoke to Elijah, kissing his cheek as she gave him a final embrace before he climbed up onto the large light grey horse he would be riding. "I will await your victorious return."

Elijah and Jeremiah were set to depart from the Kingdom of Abel, saying their goodbyes to Seth, Mary, and Benjamin at the entrance to the castle. These three were the only ones who knew of Elijah and Jeremiah's departure.

"I trust you with him," Seth said to Jeremiah, who was already mounted on his dark brown horse. "I know you will keep him safe."

"Of course, my king," Jeremiah responded as Seth turned to Elijah who was mounted up on his own horse.

"You have made me a proud father," Seth told Elijah, saying his goodbyes. "Go now in courage. Let hope guide you away from fear, and may you return to us swiftly."

"Yes, father," Elijah said, looking down to Seth who stood beside Mary and Benjamin, "I will."

Jeremiah softly kicked the sides of his horse, causing it to begin trotting forward, heading in the direction of the city gates, down the main street that was before them. Elijah did the same thing, and followed behind Jeremiah, quickly catching up to him, hidden beneath the faded moonlight that lingered over them as the city around them slept. Seth, Mary, and Benjamin, watched the two travelers as they drew further away from them down the street. The fate of the Kingdom of Abel was now resting in the hands of these two brave sons.

"You can feel it, can't you?" Seth quietly asked as Elijah and Jeremiah disappeared into the night.

"The edge of war's blade readied to strike forward?" Benjamin responded, while Mary remained silent.

"No," Seth answered, "A quest long since forgotten crying out to be remembered. The journey can no longer be avoided, nor does the reason for it need to be made. For years, the articles of this divine armor have been waiting, hidden like mice in a field, awaiting the moment of harvest when they would be taken from their hiding places. But unlike the vermin amongst the crops, left to be scattered upon being revealed, these pieces of armor will come together, and, united, have a power they did not have when divided."

"Then may they be united," Benjamin proclaimed softly, the gentle breeze blowing his long white beard from side to side, "so that our enemies be scattered."

Where East Meets Sea

Elijah and Jeremiah rode through the forest the entire night, and then stopped to rest about midday the following day, remaining under the forested region that seemed to have no end. They were traveling in an eastward direction, slightly trailing northward, where, according to the map and writings of the journal, the forest would turn to a barren land after about a week's journey on horse. After days of traveling through the barren land, they would reach the end of land, where a great body of water stood in their way of reaching the next land where they would obtain the first piece of the armor: the belt.

"We're not far off from the lake," Jeremiah said as he and Elijah sat on the rough forest ground beside a small flowing stream that was only a few feet across, and less than a foot deep, as their two horses drank from it. "We're probably less than a couple days away from it now, were we to head south-east from this point."

"This is the closest I've ever been to it," Elijah responded to Jeremiah, as Elijah lowered his back, and laid across the earth. "The furthest I've travelled away from the kingdom is to the meadow."

"I haven't travelled any further than that either," Jeremiah said, pulling out an apple from his sack of food he had brought with him, taking a bite from it as he continued the conversation with the prince. "Besides King Seth, there probably isn't anyone still alive who has gone any further away from the kingdom than the meadow. Nobody has ever needed to, for as far back as our history records. Everything we have ever needed has been less than a couple days away into the surrounding forests."

"It's a bit depressing really," Elijah spoke, his excitement for the journey stirred up like sand beneath a rushing wave. "I mean, think about it. Who knows how far the land goes? And then, according to the journal, a body of water that stretches as far as the land does. The journal calls it a 'sea.' After that, land appears again. What if all these other lands are filled with other people? We would have never known had we just stayed in the land of our fathers."

"The land of our fathers is safe," Jeremiah said, chewing with an open mouth as he continued to chat. "Why leave when everything we've ever needed is there?"

"And yet here we are, travelling to foreign lands because it doesn't have what we now need," Elijah retorted. "Trying to find a scattered weapon that's as far as possible from the kingdom, in every direction."

"Well," Jeremiah said, gnawing at the core of the apple he had devoured, spitting out the several seeds it had, "perhaps times have changed."

"I wonder what we will see in these other places," Elijah said, closing his eyes, beginning to dose off. "The journal doesn't give details about the lands that hold the pieces of armor. It only says the land is there. Maybe I will begin recording these travels as the first king did."

"You truly are an offspring of that forest settlement," Jeremiah yawned, tossing the remains of the apple away, and lying down across the ground. "You have an unquenchable hunger for discovery and exploration."

Their conversation then ended, and the two fell asleep beneath the covering of the forest, sleeping until dusk that evening. Once the sun began to set, they ate a small amount of food, and continued on their way through the forest. For the next few days, the scenery seemed to repeat itself, as they rode through the forest, passing by the same types of trees, rocks, moss, and terrain. They rarely came across any wildlife, and the few birds they did see were not new to them. Elijah kept the journal of the first king in his leather bag of supplies, and as the days in the forest went by, he would read more of it every time they stopped to rest. Instead of skipping around, and reading the parts he would find more interesting, he disciplined himself to read the journal from beginning to end. Little did Elijah know that the travels of the king into the area of the forest, where the village settlement would be birthed generations later, were recorded in this journal.

"The forest's end!" Elijah called to Jeremiah as they were travelling at a constant speed on their horses, Elijah riding about fifteen feet ahead of Jeremiah.

In the distance, a plain could be seen past the trees about a quarter mile in front of the travelers. The sun was shining brightly out there, its rays of light piercing through the gaps between trees, striking at Elijah and Jeremiah, and as the two drew closer, their eyes were able to slowly adjust to the brightness they had been shielded from in the dense forest.

"Don't rush ahead without me," Jeremiah cautiously said, catching up beside Elijah, "there's no telling what is out there. I feel as though we've been fortunate to have not encountered danger yet."

Soon enough, the two broke free from the seemingly endless forest, and made it to the clearing. Before them was an empty plain of rocky soil, as far as their eyes could see. There were no trees, streams, plant life, or even weeds across this barren land.

"Wait," Jeremiah said to Elijah, as Jeremiah caused his horse to come to a halt, slid off of it, and jogged toward one of the trees on the outskirts of the forest that was only several feet behind him.

The tree Jeremiah ran up to was only about twice his height, and unlike the other trees nearby it, this tree was dead. Not a single leaf was left on it, and its grey bark and branches had no life left in them. Hidden beneath the soil Jeremiah stood on were its roots, which no longer took drink from the faithful rain that always came to the forests.

"What are you doing?" Elijah asked him as Jeremiah pulled a small knife from his belt, and cut off a long strip of material from the sleeve of his tunic that was made of thick maroon colored wool.

"This will be the last time we are this close to home for an uncertain length of time," Jeremiah said as he tightly tied the material to a branch on the tree. "It's a faint chance we will remember exactly how to return home after this long journey. I hope to return the way we came. This will guide us home."

The piece of maroon cloth gently swayed in the wind as Jeremiah looked to it for a moment, turning away to remount his horse before his buried emotions could attempt to resurface and show that they still existed. Even within his deepest of depths, despite the rough exterior Jeremiah had developed to hide them from others, his emotions most certainly still existed.

Though with his eyes he only saw a tattered piece of material, in his heart he saw the faces of the family members he abandoned in hopes to protect them, and the city walls he never thought he would spend a night outside of. In truth, had he or Elijah been given the option, they would never have chosen the circumstances they were currently in, but this was no time to cower away from the task at hand, the road they walked. All they knew, they had left behind, and what lay before them was the unknown; uncertainty was the only thing that was certainly ahead. This was a journey not their own.

It was in this moment that Jeremiah found within him a hope to bring honor to his father's name by leading a successful journey, its success measured by protecting the prince, and playing his role in rescuing the Kingdom of Abel when they were to return with the royal armor.

Many hours went by as they tirelessly travelled through the open land, their horses at a trot that was beginning to slowly decrease in speed.

"This is so peculiar," Elijah said as they continued on under the blazing sun, the sunrays scratching at their skin that had come to appreciate the shade of the forest. "I've never seen something so void and empty before."

"It will only help us to see danger coming from a great distance," Jeremiah said back as they galloped across the empty plain.

"You worry over nothing," Elijah said back to Jeremiah.

"I was entrusted to protect you," Jeremiah spoke. "I would

be a fool to let my guard down, especially in places none of our people have ever been to. Away from home, and in these times of war, the potential for danger is in our midst."

"I won't doubt the possibility for danger," Elijah seemed to agree, "but I don't see danger coming in the form of an enemy who wields a sword, but instead in the form of thirsting to death in this endless barren land that provides no water or shade."

"May the One we serve provide us with shade and drink soon," Jeremiah said as sweat dripped down his smooth face, gathering on the bottom of his chin, and dripping onto the bushy main of his horse.

"It will be provided for us when we need it most," Elijah wisely said, encouraging the both of them to continue on, trusting that the voice that sounded from the sky to the author of the book Elijah was guarding would keep them, and give them safe passage.

As they travelled another few miles, in the distance they could see black rain clouds filling the sky, as the sun that was now beating down on them from behind, in the west, was nearing its time to set again in the next few hours.

"This may cause us trouble," Jeremiah said as they continued to travel toward the gathering rain clouds.

From where they rode, they saw streaks of flashing lightning wrapping around the black clouds in patterns that could not be figured out or reproduced. Sheets of falling rain were becoming visible, waving around in the atmosphere between earth and cloud.

"If that storm comes toward us, or if we reach it, we will have no shelter from it," Jeremiah said. "Perhaps we should pause, and see what direction this storm is moving."

"No," Elijah said, sensing a peace calling from within the storm, "we will be safe."

"We will be soaked," Jeremiah argued.

"Trust me," Elijah said calmly. "We will be fine."

Agitated, Jeremiah continued on at the normal pace his horse was at. Memories of his younger brother, Micah, crossed his mind as he found similarities between Micah's personality and Elijah's, most of which were qualities he had little patience for.

"Were you anyone else," Jeremiah said, attempting to compose himself, and keep from sounding angry, "I would have forced you to stop, but we will continue."

As they came closer to the storm clouds that remained over the same plot of land ahead of them, the storm only intensified, with lightning flashing brighter with each lightning bolt that seemed to shatter across the black rolling clouds, and the thunder that crackled from inside of the clouds only became louder, with no gaps in between its crushing sounds.

Unexpectedly, when the travelers became about a mile from the beginning of the storm, a fierce wind began to blow high in the air, causing the clouds to disperse, and spread evenly over the sky, turning from solid black to shades of light grey and blue. The lightning disappeared, the thundering became silent, and not a single drop of rain was left to fall.

As Elijah and Jeremiah rode onward, the shade the clouds brought gave comfort to their burning skin, and cooled them and their horses down. The powerful wind that obliterated the storm turned to a constant cool breeze, bringing more ease to the party.

"This cannot be," Jeremiah shockingly said, realizing his doubt had nearly kept him from reaching this peaceful point of the journey through the barren land.

"Look ahead!" Elijah said, lifting one of his hands to point toward a wide body of water that was laying in the ground further ahead of them, and beside the water was a row of massive flattened boulders. "The storm has left behind a source of water for us!"

A sudden burst of energy filled the horses, and they quickly increased their speed, pushing their way toward the body of water, thrusting thick mud, which was caused by the rainstorm, up high, staining as high as up to the horses' kneecaps.

Immediately, upon reaching the massive puddle of rain water, the horses lowered their heads, and lapped up water into their mouths, their dry tongues regaining moisture, making the bags of food and weapons strapped to their backs seem to feel lighter. As they did this, Elijah and Jeremiah climbed off of their horses, landing in the deep mud, their boots sinking two inches beneath the watery surface. Using much of their strength to trek through the soaked ground, they reached the water beside their horses, gathered water with their cupped hands, and lifted their hands to their chapped lips to finally rehydrate.

Relief fell over them. After enough gulps, Jeremiah and Elijah walked to the flat rocks that were sticking out of the mud beside the water, climbed onto them, and laid their backs to the cooled rocks, now fully able to take a rest from the barren land's terrible environment. Not yet satisfied, the horses continued to drink.

"How much more of this dead land do we have to travel across?" Jeremiah asked Elijah, nearly out of breath.

"I'm not exactly sure," Elijah answered, recalling the map he had seen sketched in the journal. "This barren land is not nearly as long as the forest. It's about a quarter of the length of the forest, so most likely a couple days."

They continued to lie there as the evening came and went. Nightfall arrived, turning the land nearly pitch-black with the clouds partially concealing the stars and moon high above the empty land. Elijah and Jeremiah's exhausted bodies did not move from their place on the rocks, and their horses stayed beside the rocks, resting in the cold mud.

Elijah stood in the middle of a great battlefield, dressed in the armor of an eastern warrior. He looked down to see the ground of the earth tilled over, creating a mix of churned mud decorated with ash and soot. He looked above to see random puffs of black smoke scattered across the atmosphere not much higher than his own head, the smoke seeming to take on the shapes of people in horrific poses as if they were fleeing, or shielding themselves from being attacked. Above the dark smoke, Elijah's eyes caught onto the sight of a white eagle gliding across the air, not calling out from its beak, only observing the destruction below.

Turning his head toward one direction, he saw a huge crowd of men dressed in armor from the Kingdom of Abel. The whole group of these men stood in silence, and they were looking directly at Elijah. Confused, Elijah silently looked back at them, looking to their faces that were drained of energy.

Suddenly, an odd feeling struck Elijah, and he turned around to see his father, King Seth, walking toward him, with the two eastern Diadem following behind him. Seth looked much younger than how Elijah now knew him, but he was still able to recognize him, especially because he carried the king's staff in his hand, and wore the crown of gold and opal on his head. Seth's eyes were lowered, almost looking down toward Elijah's feet.

"Father?" Elijah called out to Seth, but his father ignored

him, walking past Elijah, continuing on toward his army.

Out of nowhere, a flock of red-orange birds with black speckles across their bodies shot past Elijah, coming from his left side, striking at him with a surprisingly forceful wind. Elijah looked to his right, in the direction the birds had flown, to see the silhouette of a man kneeling on the ground in front of a small hole, with the dirt dug up to make this hole piled around it. The man was at a distance to where Elijah could barely make out his figure, the hole, and the dirt around it. The flock of birds was shooting off into the forest behind the man.

The unidentifiable man stretched his arms out over the small piles of dirt, and began to push the dirt into the hole, refilling it. Once all the dirt was back in the hole, the man began to push the dirt down, pressing it back into the earth, one forceful push at a time, and with each push, the ground beneath Elijah shook extremely violently, as though an army had gathered beneath the earth's surface, and were striking at the surface in rhythm with the man pushing against the earth. Elijah felt like he was on the inside of a beating drum.

After three violent shakes, Elijah was thrown to the ground, and once his body hit the ground, banging came from beneath the earth's surface, as though the army below lost their rhythm, and were all striking the earth at their own pace and preference. The chaotic pounding that was coming from every direction became louder and louder, gaining in intensity with every pound, tossing Elijah from side to side.

All of the sudden, hundreds of hands and arms broke out from beneath the earth, black armor visible from their wrists down. One hand that had come up to Elijah's right side grabbed onto his shoulder, and tightly shook him, Elijah's fear exploding nearly as loud as the shout that was coming from his mouth.

A scream came out of Elijah's mouth as his upper body shot up from its stretched out position over the long flat rock in the barren land.

"Elijah!" Jeremiah loudly said, his hand tightly gripped onto Elijah's right shoulder.

Extremely disturbed and disoriented, Elijah swatted at Jeremiah's hand, causing him to let go of Elijah as Elijah regained consciousness, remembering he was in the barren land, and realizing the terror he had just seen was only a nightmare.

"Elijah?" Jeremiah repeated his name, this time confused with what was happening.

"I'm sorry," Elijah apologized.

"Were you dreaming?" Jeremiah asked Elijah as Elijah wiped his face, the rising sun becoming visible in the east, revealing the thin clouds still hovering above them and the water that was slowly sinking beneath the mud.

"Yes," Elijah responded, "I dream often."

"Your mind knows no rest," Jeremiah told him, as Elijah took in a deep breath.

"I don't think my dreams are just my imagination running boundless," Elijah said, rubbing the crust away from around his eyes. "I think they give me insight to things past, and foresight for things that have not yet happened."

"Enough of this," Jeremiah said, standing to his feet on the rock, and putting his hand out to help Elijah stand up as well. "We don't need to waste our time talking about what you see when your eyes are closed, and how it could be significant. Enough dreaming."

"They are not just dreams," Elijah responded back aggressively, not reaching his hand out to Jeremiah, and remaining in his same position on the rock. "I think they are closer to reality."

"This, right now, is reality," Jeremiah said, pulling his hand away from the prince, spreading his arms out from his sides. "This barren land, and our journey through it, is reality. The war that is being waged, even when we are away, is reality. And what's worse is the reality that all our loved ones, and our home, are in grave danger while we are gone for this next year. Anything could happen in this world you are awake in; the only difference between it and your dreams is that you won't wake up from it when everything begins to go wrong. The terror of this life won't be erased by opening your eyes."

"Have you lost sight of hope?" Elijah loudly asked back to Jeremiah as he stood on his feet with his own strength.

"It's only a fool's hope if you sit and do nothing, waiting for things to work out!" Jeremiah yelled at Elijah, turning his back to him to begin walking off the rocks, his heavy boots landing in the mud that was much drier than the day before.

A brief pause fell over them as Elijah stood still on the rocks, watching Jeremiah gather rainwater from a puddle into his flask.

"You would still be dying of thirst in this land had I not had hope that we would be divinely taken care of on this journey," Elijah angrily said, unable to end the disagreement, his feet frozen on the rock, not moving at all.

"And you, Elijah," Jeremiah began to say, holding back the anger in his voice behind his teeth as he pushed the cork back into his tin flask that was now full, "would have no hope on this journey without me to defend you."

No more words were exchanged as the two prepared to leave, and continued through the barren land, riding on their horses, able to drink from their filled flasks as they went, sharing enough water with their horses to keep them able to travel. The thin clouds that blocked most of the deadly heat of the sun followed over them, making their travel much less exhausting.

On horse, they travelled until the sun sat again, and they slept on the rough ground of the empty land for the night, beneath the stars and moonlight that became very bright, because once the sun sat in the west, the clouds disappeared.

As the two laid still in the comfortable weather of this desert's night, Elijah could no longer take the silence.

"Who are they?" Elijah questioned into the night air, his voice gently meeting Jeremiah's ears.

"Who are who, Elijah?" Jeremiah responded calmly to the prince, his temper cooled down drastically from the last time they had spoken.

"The ones you fight for," Elijah continued. "The loved ones you miss back home that you fear for in your absence. Do you mean your family?"

"Well," Jeremiah answered, still laying on his side, his back toward Elijah's body, while Elijah was lying on his back and looking to the stars that were shining brighter than he had ever seen in his life. "Yes. My mother and my six brothers. They are dear to me, and I have always had to be there for them. My father died years ago, in the battle for the forest village."

"He died defending my people," Elijah spoke, their two bodies lying still against the cooled earth, "and my parents."

"Yes," Jeremiah said, "and you as well."

"I have heard stories of his bravery," Elijah spoke. "He must have been an honorable warrior."

"One of the most courageous of his time," Jeremiah added.

"Do you remember him well?" Elijah asked.

"I remember him being one of the lead generals over the eastern military," Jeremiah said. "Though he fell in battle, he is responsible for one of the greatest victories in that battle."

"My people were all killed," Elijah responded upset. "What victory is there to remember from that battle?"

"He's the man who safely delivered you to the east," Jeremiah reluctantly answered.

Complete silence fell over the two for the next few moments. Seth had never revealed to Elijah who, by name, had delivered him to Mary, causing Elijah to now be speechless with Jeremiah delivering him this information.

"I am eternally grateful for his act of bravery," Elijah said, turning his face toward Jeremiah's broad back that was still facing him.

"I only hope to be as great a warrior as he was," Jeremiah said, staring blankly into the endless land that faded into black, far away from where he watched.

"You have been given the same task as him: to safely see me

through until I reach the Kingdom of Abel." Elijah encouragingly responded. "I'm sure you will prove to be his son."

Silence came over the two, but it took much time before either of them could fall asleep because of the emotions that were stirred up from their conversation. Elijah lay there, almost in guilt over the way he had spoken to Jeremiah earlier because he had lost his father over protecting Elijah, as though Elijah were in debt to this guardian. In Jeremiah's mind, thoughts of insecurity due to his inability to think that he could truly live up to his father's status were drowning him, along with the pain of a wound over the loss of his father that had never healed.

"Father?" Jeremiah, as a child, squeaked out, standing in the front room of the house he and his family lived in.

It was so early that the sun had not even begun to rise, but Jeremiah had been woken up by the sound of his father, Mareshah, putting on his heavy armor moments ago.

Mareshah, standing at the front door, about to walk out, turned back to see his oldest son watching him about to leave.

"Jeremiah." Mareshah smiled, walking up to Jeremiah, and kneeling down, the top of Maresha's head becoming about level with his son's, allowing their eyes to look into each other. "What are you doing up this early?"

"I heard you getting dressed," Jeremiah answered as Mareshah sat his large hands onto Jeremiah's frail shoulders. "I thought you were back home from fighting?"

"I was," Mareshah explained, happy to see his son before leaving. "But the battle is still not over. I have to go back until it's finished."

"Then why did you leave in the middle of it?" Jeremiah asked, really only asking more questions to have more time with his father.

"I had to bring something to the queen," Mareshah creatively explained. "A very special present that we brought back to her from the forest."

"Did the present make her happy?" Jeremiah asked more.

"Yes," Mareshah joyfully said to his son, "it did."

"Can you bring me a present, too?" Jeremiah asked, causing his father to chuckle.

"I'll see what I can do," Mareshah said, embracing his son, his strong arms wrapping around Jeremiah.

"Don't go," Jeremiah said, a frown striking across his lips, his small arms grabbing onto the metal armor across his father's back, holding tighter onto his father now than if he had the arms of a full-grown man.

"I have to, my son," Mareshah said, his joy being mixed with sorrow over having to leave his family.

"Then take me with you," Jeremiah began to cry.

"I will be back," Mareshah said, kissing his son on the forehead. "We will be together, again."

Mareshah released himself from the hug with his son to see the many tears coming down Jeremiah's face. With his rough fingertips, he began to wipe away the tears from Jeremiah's sensitively soft cheeks, while Maresha himself fought back tears at seeing his son heartbroken over his departure.

"Take care of your brothers, and your mother while I am gone," Mareshah told his son, smiling at Jeremiah, hiding his own sadness. "Especially your new baby brother, Micah."

"I will," Jeremiah began to sniffle, his breaths short and quick.

"You will be a greater warrior than even me, one day," Mareshah humbly told his boy, standing up onto his feet.

Jeremiah looked up at his father, dressed in the fine armor of the Kingdom of Abel, his shoulders wide and his chest outward. The finely carved emblem of the olive tree on his father's breastplate would be a symbol that would never leave Jeremiah's memories.

With this, Mareshah turned his back to his son, and walked toward the front door, two heavy tears cascading down from his dark brown eyes, the emotion concealed from his son as he opened the door, walked out, and closed it behind him, not turning his face back toward his son.

Jeremiah suddenly opened his eyes wide to see the endless barren land he had seen before falling asleep, now revealed in the morning sunlight. The dream he had just had was one that would haunt him from time to time, reminding him of his last moments with his father.

He sat up, and looked behind him to see Elijah pealing off the skin of an orange that came from his sack of food.

"Would you like a piece?" Elijah asked Jeremiah, pulling apart a skinned piece of the orange, and holding it out to Jeremiah.

"Thank you," Jeremiah said, taking the wet slice, and eating it, giving moisture and sweet flavor to his dry and distasteful mouth.

After this small breakfast, the two continued on their way through the void land. At about noontime, they came up to a point in the land where the ground went from being completely flat, to a sharp hillside incline that went at least a dozen times as high as their heads from where they sat on their obedient horses. Noise of what sounded like crashing and shouting of countless warriors in the far distance on the other side of this mound filled their ears.

"What's that noise?" Elijah asked as Jeremiah slid off of his horse, and jogged up to the incline. "It sounds like an army. Could the west be assembling this far east?"

"I will investigate before we cross over this risen mound of earth," Jeremiah swiftly spoke, pulling his sword out from his sheath, and crawling up the high hill. "Stay here."

Elijah watched Jeremiah climb up the hill, and once he reached the top, peaked over to see what the source of the commotion was. He stared over the hill's top for several seconds before silently pulling his whole body over onto the top of the mound, and stood on it, facing toward the roaring sounds, his hair thrashing ferociously in the wind that was blowing at his front side. His tight grip loosened, causing the sword to fall from his hand.

"Jeremiah!" Elijah called to him, frightened and confused at what was happening. "What do you see? How many of them are there?"

"Come see for yourself," Jeremiah said, turning to Elijah, and then turning back to whatever it was he was looking at, his clothing being blown just as wildly as his hair.

Riding his horse, Elijah cautiously rode up the mound with Jeremiah's horse following behind him. Once he reached the top, amazement struck the jaw-dropped prince.

Before them, beginning at the bottom of the opposite side of his hill, was about one hundred more feet of earth, but, unlike the rocky ground they walked on, it was covered with sand the color of harvested wheat and snow. At the end of the stretch of sand were massive waves of sea crashing against the shore, roaring like an endless army of warriors readied for battle, the waves pounding against the sands with the force of falling stars. They had never seen anything like this. None of their people had ever seen a sea, or even imagined anything like it.

"This is the sea!" Elijah said, kicking at his horse's sides, causing it to creep down the mound, and enter onto the sandy beach.

It was very windy, and a heavy fog could be seen over the sea in the distance. There were grey clouds filling the atmosphere of this entire area, causing the temperature to be much cooler than in the barren land they had left on the other side of the mound.

Jeremiah and his horse reached the sands, following behind the prince and his horse, kicking up sand in every direction as they ran through it. Elijah quickly jumped off of his horse, and got only a few feet from the waves hitting the shore, chunks of wet sand clinging onto his boots.

"This is amazing!" Elijah happily said, excited by this discovery, witnessing something nobody from his kingdom had ever seen.

The two men stood entranced by the ocean, its magnificent sight and sounds sketching memories they would forever remember into their thoughts.

Jeremiah watched as the horses walked up to small puddles of gathered seawater in the sand near the waves, and drank from them. Jeremiah walked over to one himself, and began to drink from it too. The water was clear as the sky, and tasted very sweet and refreshing.

"We were cursed with thirst these past days," Jeremiah said as Elijah walked up to him, "now we have more water than we could ever drink."

Elijah cupped up water from the same puddle as Jeremiah, and took a drink.

"In all this amazement, I am left with one question," Jeremiah said, turning back to the untamed sea. "How are we to cross it?"

Elijah, coming back to realization of the task at hand, looked back to the sea, its unruly waves smashing against the passive shore, taking every hit and never striking back. Neither he nor Jeremiah had any clue as to how to travel over this sea to reach the land where the belt was waiting for them.

Passage to Terrabeth

After reaching the sea, Elijah and Jeremiah camped out there for the night, falling asleep on the beach side of the foot of the steep hill. They faced the mound to shield their faces from the strong wind that was blowing at them as their bodies shook while they laid balled up, trying to keep warm, unable to make a fire because there was no dry brush around. For their journey, Jeremiah had packed, into their supply bags, rocks to spark up a fire, but these tools were useless now.

Though he was very cold, Jeremiah fell asleep quickly, leaving Elijah awake under the bright moonlight. The moon seemed to find just the right spot between clouds to settle, and light up the waves which had come to a near standstill on the shore, with the softest of waves brushing onto the sand.

A faint high-pitched wailing began to call out from the waters, causing Elijah to quietly roll over, and turn toward the sea. Without waking up his protector, Elijah stood, listening to the new sound that seemed to be more like a familiar song than a foreign cry, which was drawing Elijah out to where it came from.

With his arms folded across his chest, trying to keep warm, Elijah slowly walked toward the waters of the sea, the bright moonlight reflecting itself off the waters like a shifting mirror, concealing whatever it was that was making the sounds that continued to go on. Elijah's tunic flapped violently in the wind, whipping the air as it did, with his hair being forced away from his forehead.

As he continued to walk, Elijah began to realize what song this was, and he began to sing wordless notes along to it, the tune seeping out of his shivering lips. It was the song of hope: Psalm of the East.

Once Elijah reached the water's edge, he came to a pause, and clouds began to move in front of the moon, blocking its view of what was happening on the shore, stripping away the moonlight that was shimmering across the top of the sea, causing the place where Elijah stood to become nearly pitch black. At this, Elijah did not hesitate to remain where he stood, finding a peace with the song, entranced by its clarity, eager to find its source. The weak incoming waves brushed against the bottom of his brown boots, foaming around his hidden feet.

In the darkness, Elijah began to squint his eyes to see faint lights of faded blue, purple, and green beginning to appear beneath the surface of the sea, far out from where he stood. There were multiple sources emitting these lights, and with this, Elijah realized it was not one source that this song was coming from, but multiple sources that were all slowly moving around, grouped together. Without realizing it, Elijah began to join the song more loudly, astonished at the beautiful chorus of this choir of lights that were reflecting a dance across the sea's top.

Certain lights became wider and brighter as their sources neared the surface of the water, revealing the massive size of each source of light, and before these lights faded away, going back to lower depths, puffs of steam and water shot out from them, reaching high up into the air, but Elijah stood still with no fear.

Without warning, the lights began to drift away from where they were hiding, swimming further out into the sea, leaving Elijah behind. His voice became softer and softer as the singing lights became more faint, their songs fading away in the distance. Within moments, Elijah was left in silence again, staring out toward the lights that had disappeared, and the song that had fallen quiet.

The following day, Elijah and Jeremiah remained at this campsite, unsure of how to cross the sea whose sight was no longer a stranger to them. Elijah kept secret what he had seen the night before, fearful that Jeremiah's doubt would cause him to not believe Elijah's story of what he had witnessed. That occurrence, though mostly unexplainable, had brought much peace to Elijah, and he was not willing to forfeit that by its memory being joined with an argument over if it had truly happened, or if it could have been a trap that Elijah had fallen victim to, giving away their whereabouts to the western army.

As their quest continued on, back home in the Kingdom of Abel, King Seth patiently waited for his son and captain to return home. The spies stationed along the fog barrier, and at the eastern lake, had not reported any sightings of the western military. Though on the edge of attack, things appeared to be very calm, as if the kingdom were in the eye of a destructive hurricane that was ready to come back over them in great terror.

During the days when Elijah and Jeremiah had first left, the entire city had been on edge, ready to have their kingdom threatened at any moment, but because of the lack of violence in over a week, the people were beginning to return back to their daily routines, forgetting the risk their lives were in.

In the west, Olivia was biding her time, trying to scheme a flawless attack to tear down the reign of her father in the east, and finish what she had set out to do over sixteen years ago: slay Elijah.

Though Plague was the most powerful of beasts in the land, he could not be touched by the light of day, so he was bound to the west for the time being, dwelling under its shadows of constant night. Because of the lack of violence for those in the west, they became more restless, ready to finally attack and destroy the kingdom they had rebelled against.

Night once more fell over the shore where Elijah and Jeremiah remained stuck. In the day to follow, they walked up and down the sandy shore, only to find its scenery was as monotonous as the barren land they had just escaped from. Their red burnt skin that had cooled at first in the cold wind was now becoming irritated as the relentless wind scratched at their tired bodies, tossing sand all over them. Even though their journey seemed to be on pause, they could not escape the constant ware their bodies were forced to endure. Exhausted, and drained of energy, the two returned to their campsite to sleep for the night.

Near dawn, the high pitched sounds that had woken Elijah began to call out again from the sea, causing Elijah to wake up, with the sky over the sea beginning to warm up to brighter shades of blue, though the sun had still yet to peer over the smoothly moving waves.

Elijah squinted his eyes, looking toward the sea, while the strong bursts of wind tossed bits of sand into his hair that had become very greasy. His black hair took hold of the grainy sand as Jeremiah rolled over, facing toward the sea as well.

"What is that noise?" Jeremiah groaned, confused at the sound that seemed to be far off.

Elijah, without a response, stood up, and began to walk toward the sea. The high-pitched noise was not singing the eastern ballad this time, but instead the many voices seemed to be calling out for attention. On the horizon of the sea, a large figure floating on the water, shadowed by the birthing sunlight behind it, became visible.

"Do you see that?" Elijah said loudly, as Jeremiah quickly got onto his feet, and walked up beside Elijah, "riding on the waves, like a swan of some sort."

"It seems to be crying out," Jeremiah added, the rim of the sun beginning to shine behind it as the figure continued to slowly creep toward the shore. "Maybe it is an animal of some sort. I've never seen anything like it. It could be dangerous."

"No," Elijah spoke, "those singing voices, I heard them the other night. They came close to shore."

"This creature came close to you?" Jeremiah asked. "Where was I?"

"You were sleeping," Elijah answered as the figure unnoticeably drew closer. "It was multiple voices, and they were beneath the surface of the water. I couldn't see what they were."

"Well just as many calls are sounding now," Jeremiah said looking back to Elijah, "but there is only one creature that I can see."

"They were singing Psalm of the East," Elijah said. "Whatever it is, I don't think it is bringing us any harm."

"Why didn't you tell me about any of this?" Jeremiah asked confused, causing Elijah to look him in the eyes.

"Would you have believed my account without seeing it for yourself?" Elijah softly answered, causing a brief silence to fall, followed by the two looking back to the ocean to see the figure drawing closer, though it was still a great distance away.

Another hour passed before the figure drew close enough for the two men to see what it was, though it was something they had never before seen. It was a massive wooden ship, with wide sails spread out over it, guiding the ship toward the shore by means of the fierce wind racing over the sea. The exterior of the ship was painted over in a gloss that made the rose colored wood much more vibrant, calling much attention to the fine craftsmanship that had been used in the construction of this vehicle. Bursts of steam shot up spontaneously from the seawater surrounding the ship, with the crying sounds still singing out without a rhythm to their melodies.

Elijah and Jeremiah remained standing on the edge of the shore as this giant foreign object, nearly one hundred feet away from them now, cut through the waves, like a knife through warm butter, while the winds kicked at the back of the sails, thrusting the ship toward the sandy shore.

Unexpectedly, the wind began to change course, causing the ship to turn north, leaving it to sail parallel with the shoreline, about fifty feet offshore. As it did this, the wind began to quickly die away, and the ship came to a light drift, hardly moving at all.

From where they stood still, Elijah burst out into a sprint, racing after the ship, running parallel with it, staying on the muddy sand, but not stepping into the water.

"Elijah!" Jeremiah yelled, running after the prince.

Once the two caught up to the ship that was still facing north, they stood still, watching from the sands. The high-pitched noises fell silent, and the steam that was shooting up around the ship ceased, leaving the beach eerily quiet.

Suddenly, several sea creatures revealed themselves from beneath the water, raising their heads, which were attached to their extremely long necks, out of the sea. Their necks reached as high up as the top of the ship's sails, and their smooth and shiny skin was the shade of a red so faded it was almost white. Planted across their necks were patterns of clear stones, and each creature had one large clear stone on its forehead. They had oval shaped heads, with long snouts that had two long nostrils which had been causing the steam to shoot up around the ship moments earlier. Each one of them had two small solid black eyes encircled by black skin, shadowing their slightly sunken eye sockets, and all their eyes were looking downward toward Elijah and Jeremiah who watched stunned from the shore.

"What beasts are these?!" Jeremiah yelled, instantly pulling his sword out of his sheath, horrified at the sheer size of these creatures.

In response, the sea creatures opened their mouths, revealing their hundreds of teeth that were round and dull, not sharp at all. From their open mouths erupted their hollering high-pitched voices, as though combating Jeremiah's threatening sword with their echoing sounds. As soon as they roared, the stones across their necks began to glow different shades of light blue, purple, and green, corresponding with the sound pattern that was coming from their own vocal chords. The stones atop their heads remained unlit.

With the intense sound waves all focused on Jeremiah, the force threw him back onto the sand, his sword flying out from his grip, while Elijah stood frozen in awe.

A whistle suddenly came from the ship, breaking through the deafening cries, forcing each creature to become silent, causing their stones to become dim. All but one of the creatures sunk their heads back beneath the ocean surface, and the one that remained elevated drifted toward the side of the ship that faced the shore.

A short man that was on the ship revealed himself as he walked toward the creature that was waiting for him. The creature lowered its head, making it level with the side of the ship, and the man climbed over the ship's side, onto the creature's head.

As Jeremiah stood back onto his feet, the short man, now standing on the creatures head, pointed toward Elijah and Jeremiah, ordering the creature to take him to them.

"Where am I?!" the short man asked excitedly as the creature drew closer to the shore. "What is this place?"

"Who are you?" Jeremiah sharply responded to the man, pulling Elijah behind his sturdy body.

"Don't worry," the man said back as the creature reached the shore, and slid onto land, revealing its massive body that had four wide flippers for appendages, and a long tail. "We mean you no harm. But tell me, where am I?"

"You are in the east," Elijah told him as the creature lowered its head to the ground, allowing the man to slide off its head, and onto the sand, "which is under the ruling of the Kingdom of Abel."

"Kingdom of Abel?" the man said back. "Though I have travelled through every land, I've never heard of such a kingdom. Who is your king?"

"King Seth," Jeremiah answered, taking the conversation away from Elijah, worrying Elijah might share too much information with this stranger. "We belong to his kingdom, and serve under his ruling. Where are you from?"

"I am from Terrabeth," the short tanned man said, looking up toward the two young men, his forehead glistening in the sun. "My name is Royce. I am a traveler who explores the many lands and seas of this world. But, never have I discovered an uncharted land!"

"Wait," Elijah interrupted, "many lands of this world? You know of other lands?"

"Yes," Royce answered. "I know of all of them. Or, at least I thought I did."

"We need your help," Elijah began to explain.

"Elijah, stop," Jeremiah spouted out, putting his hand on Elijah's chest. "For all we know he is a spy from the west."

"I am no spy," Royce abruptly stated, as his straight blonde hair that rested just above his eyebrows began to calmly sway with the wind, "I assure you of that. I rarely even speak with other people. I have my songvissen. They are all the company I need."

Royce was referring to the sea creatures that accompanied him as he travelled across the seas. In his separation from other people, he found affection in their loyalty, and peace in their song. The songvis that brought him to the shore patiently sat on the sand, waiting for further instructions from its master.

"I trust you," Elijah said in desperation for aid from Royce, who was a few years older than Jeremiah.

Elijah lifted his hand onto Royce's shoulder, which was almost level with Elijah's, and Royce's heart seemed to sink deeper into his chest, like a smooth stone tossed down a dried well, banging against the stone walls its whole way down.

"You have my word," Royce spoke frailly, "I am no spy."

"We need your help," Elijah began to explain, removing his

hand from Royce's shoulder, while Jeremiah silently listened. "Our kingdom is in great danger. I must reach several other lands before I return home if there is any hope."

"Where must you go?" Royce enquired. "You don't even need to tell me why. I want to help you, and prove to you I am no spy."

Elijah then still explained what had happened to the Kingdom of Abel, telling most of the story, leaving out the fact of his royal title, and the journal he kept with him.

"I will help you save your kingdom," Royce agreed.

With that, Elijah and Jeremiah gathered all their belongings from their campsite on the beach, excluding the horses. Then, climbed onto the songvis that transported Royce from the ship to the shore, had it float them to the ship's side, and the three men boarded it.

Walking onto the ship, Elijah and Jeremiah saw a huge sketch painted on the front deck. It was an outline of the lands and seas of the world, with each continent and body of water labeled by name. Elijah immediately recognized it, having seen it in the journal he had been studying. After further observation, Elijah noticed that the land that the Kingdom of Abel was on was not included in the map Royce had drawn. At the center of the map, where Elijah's home continent should have been, was only an open sea. The several other continents were far away from his homeland, surrounding it from every direction, as though they were all at attention before this divine and secret continent, circling around it.

"Here," Elijah said, kneeling down over the continent labeled Terrabeth on the map, which was northeast from where they were now, "this is where we must go first."

"So we will be leaving your homeland for my own," Royce said, looking from the map on the wooden floor, out to the seemingly endless sea. "I just don't know how to get there, because I don't know where we are."

"Do you have any more paint for your map?" Elijah spoke to Royce, standing back up, while Jeremiah stood on the edge of the ship, looking to the songvissen that were gracefully gliding in the water.

"Here," Royce said, pulling out a broken piece of white chalk from a pocket in his dark blue tunic, "this is what I have left."

Elijah knelt back down, and then slowly drew the outline of his home continent, the faint sound of the dragging chalk that was shortening in the hands of Elijah was drowned out by the waves that were beginning to pick up again.

"This is where we are," Elijah said, writing 'Kingdom of Abel,' within the body of land he had just drawn, and then pointed at the eastern edge of the land, at about the location where they currently were.

"I have discovered a new land after all!" Royce said excitedly. "You must tell me all about your land. I imagine it must be very different, since it is unknown by the rest of the known world."

"I will tell you as much as I know about it," Elijah said as Jeremiah walked up beside him. "But first we must be on our way. I imagine it will take at least two weeks to reach Terrabeth."

"At least a month," Royce corrected him.

"We only have enough food for a little more than one week," Jeremiah said, finally joining the conversation, still frustrated that Elijah ignorantly formed an alliance with a stranger in this time of war.

"I have plenty of food," Royce offered, eager to gain their trust. "You can take as much as you like. You are welcome to everything on this ship. It is everything I own."

"Thank you," Elijah said with relief as Jeremiah beamed his gaze onto Royce's face, attempting to see beneath his exterior.

"It has been years since I have spoken this much with another person," Royce admitted. "I must say, I have missed interaction with others."

The wind then picked up much more forcefully, filling the sails, leading the ship in a northeast direction.

"My," Royce said, walking to the front edge of the ship,

seeing the songvissen joyfully splashing and darting through the water, moving in the same direction as the ship, "the wind is already taking us where you need to go. It seems that chance is in your favor."

"There is no such thing as chance where we come from," Elijah said, walking to Royce's side as Jeremiah stood still at the same spot, trying to keep his balance with the rocking ship. "We are being guided by something greater than chance."

Within hours, the ship had sailed so far northeast that they lost sight of the beach, and the team was now fully out at sea. The songvissen calmly travelled alongside the ship, as they always had with Royce, gently singing as they did.

Soon, night fell, and Elijah and Royce found themselves up late talking with each other on the deck of the ship, looking up to the oceans of stars above them, riding the seas of water beneath them. They seemed to have a lot in common, but Royce had a distance about him still that kept him from fully opening up. His conversation with Elijah and Jeremiah through their first day together was only about his explorations to the different lands. It never got deeper than this when he spoke. His privacy in speaking about his past was only outmatched by Jeremiah's caution to share the same about himself. Jeremiah barely spoke the entire day, and even ate very little of the food offered to him.

"How long until we will see land again?" Elijah asked him as the two sat on the edge of the front of the ship, their four legs dangling off the ship's edge, feeling frozen by the cold sea air the ship was pushing through as it travelled at a moderate speed.

"Before reaching the mainland of Terrabeth, we will pass by a series of small islands that are a day's travel or less away from the mainland," Royce shared with Elijah. "They are simply called the Daughters of Terrabeth, and they are an extension of Terrabeth. We will only pass by them though, and sail on toward the mainland, otherwise, this trip would become even longer."

"We must do nothing that will cause the trip to last longer," Elijah quickly said to Royce.

"We won't," Royce said, the wind blowing his hair away from his face, and causing Elijah's hair to become frizzy. "I know you want to save your kingdom before it's too late. I will do all I can to return you home with the least amount of time spent on anything other than your goal of obtaining the six pieces of armor."

"You've travelled this world," Elijah said as he and Royce looked down to the dark ocean to see the lights of the songvissen dimly reflecting from beneath the moving waters, their singing a distant echo coming from beneath the depths. "You have travelled to all these places we are going. How long will it take us?"

"To reach Terrabeth from our location would normally take about a month," Royce said, laying his back against the ship floor, supporting the back of his head with his stacked hands that were now being pressed between his thin hair and the smoothed wooden deck. "To travel to all the continents of this world where you need to go would take an additional year and a half or more."

"I've been gone from my home for weeks now," Elijah said, his eyes widening. "I fear what could have happened in that short amount of time, much less what could happen in the time you are saying this will take."

"Well," Royce said, looking up to the transparent sheet of clouds that seemed to be holding up the countless number of stars like a net in the midnight sky, "the ship can only travel as fast as the wind blows. But, even before you boarded this ship, the wind has been blowing very ferociously over the seas, as though trying to rush events into play. That's what took me to the shore where I found you. If the wind blows a certain way, I cannot help but go where it takes me. And the speed of this wind is something I've never seen, apart from a great storm developing, or in its fury."

"Do your songvissen not guide you?" Elijah asked, noticing their lights beneath the surface of water lighting up far ahead in the direction the ship was going.

"They don't guide," Royce said, closing his eyes, being comfortable in the company of his new friend, and in the cool weather of the night, "but, somehow, they always know where I am going. Sometimes, a few of them will travel far ahead of me to inspect what lies ahead."

"They came to me nights ago," Elijah breathed softly.

"Did you teach them that song?" Royce asked, not surprised that they had reached Elijah before he had. "Days ago a few of them left and returned singing a song I've never heard before. It was so peaceful, that song they sang."

"They approached me singing it," Elijah said, folding his arms across his stomach.

"They are very talented at reproducing songs they hear," Royce explained, "but, sometimes, in the silence of our words, they can hear the songs being sung within us, and they sing it out. You must have a true peace within you. Never before had I felt such calmness in hearing a song."

"Where are they from?" Elijah asked. "We have nothing like them where I come from."

"They are from where I come from," Royce spoke softly, becoming sleepy. "They mainly live around the Daughters of Terrabeth, and, for the most part, get along well with people. I have seen very few anywhere else on my travels. In every case I've come across one, the rogue songvis seen away from Terrabeth is always with a Terrabeth native. Despite those few songvissen, the rest fill our shores and waters."

"Terrabeth must be a loud place," Elijah joked.

"Oh, they'll keep you up all night on the islands from time to time," Royce chuckled, his eyes still closed, "but it's a beautiful melody to behold, accompanied by their fantastic lights that follow their song. It's one of the fondest memories of my home, and, luckily, I've never had to depart from it."

"When did you first leave Terrabeth?" Elijah continued their conversation.

"…About five years ago," Royce said, a sudden hesitation in his words, though his face did not change.

"Why did you leave?" Elijah asked, causing Royce to open his eyes, and fall back away from the slumber he was succumbing to.

"I chose to," Royce spoke. "I left on my own accord, ready to see what else this world had to offer."

"Was home not enough?" Elijah questioned, causing Royce to sit up.

"It was for a time," Royce said in a short tone, looking to Elijah who was now looking back at him.

"I didn't mean to offend you," Elijah said gently as Royce pulled his legs from the edge of the ship, and stood up.

"You didn't," Royce responded as Elijah stood up as well. "It's just very late, and I have grown tired. I am going to bed now. You are welcome to stay out here as long as you wish, until you decide to go to bed."

"I will stay out here for a while longer," Elijah said as Royce turned away, and began walking toward the opening to a stairwell at the back end of the ship that led to the many rooms below. "Goodnight."

"Goodnight," Royce responded to Elijah, as Elijah silently watched him walk away, confused at how their conversation had ended so abruptly.

As Royce walked down the steps, Elijah looked back to the sea, hearing the songvissen beginning to faintly sing out low notes that were almost sorrowful, far beneath the surface of the ocean where they were swimming.

For a moment, he thought to go read the journal, especially since he had not read it for a few days now, but he had grown tired as well, and decided to sleep instead.

Another week went by until Elijah even again thought to read the journal. He had become quite attached to Royce, so much so that Jeremiah had let his guard down, and was now no longer paranoid about Royce. Being within such close proximity for so constant of a time, they were left with nearly no other options. Elijah never asked again about Royce's departure from his homelands, and Royce's reaction in conversation that first night was never spoken about. As they travelled on toward Terrabeth, Elijah shared more about his home to Royce, and Royce shared more about his to Elijah, also teaching him how to manage the sails and the ship, so Elijah could share in tending to the ship, making sure they were sailing in the right direction. As best Royce could, he also taught Elijah how to navigate across the sea by using a brilliantly bright star that shined in the east.

In preparation for the rest of their journey, Elijah shared with Royce the other five places they needed to find the pieces of armor, and they planned an appropriate route to travel the world, obtaining these lost pieces of armor as quickly as possible. With a blade, they marked each of the sketched continents on the ship deck with a simple carving of which of the six pieces that land held. Terrabeth had a belt, Terrashin had shoes, Terravau had a breastplate, Terraresh had a shield, Terradaleth had a helmet, and the Valley of Shadow had a sword. This, as well, was the order of stops they planned to make, sailing across the world from continent to continent, circling in a counterclockwise fashion around the home continent of Elijah and Jeremiah. Along with these six continents they planned to stop at, were other continents and smaller bodies of land, but they did not plan to stop at any of them.

The full moon was shining brightly over the sea that felt as though it had no end as they travelled across it. Elijah sat on the deck, alone, while his two friends ate a late dinner below. Elijah, journal in hand, opened it up to where he had left off. He had reached a section of the journal where the first king was giving an account during the days of the kingdom's construction. Elijah was reading of the different tribes, and how each was over a certain section of the kingdom that could now be enjoyed by Elijah's generation.

"What are you reading?" Royce's voice asked, coming from Elijah's back right side.

"Nothing," Elijah responded hastily, quickly closing the book, and holding it tightly in his grasp, his fingers pressing into the worn leather covering.

"Did you find this book on my ship?" Royce questioned, as Jeremiah walked up to them.

"It's my own," Elijah responded, standing up, and turning around to face Royce and Jeremiah. "I brought it with me from home."

"It's just a silly book," Jeremiah said trying to disinterest Royce, Jeremiah's nerves about to burst at the carelessness Elijah had just displayed in keeping the journal private.

An awkward silence fell over the three of them as Royce realized the other two were keeping a secret from him.

"I will respect your privacy," Royce sternly spoke. "I only expect you do the same for me... I'm returning downstairs to finish eating."

Royce walked away, leaving Jeremiah to stare down Elijah

with an intimidating glance that was silently rebuking him.

"I will join you," Jeremiah called out to Royce, breaking his stare with Elijah, and walking after Royce.

After that, Elijah hid the journal away, and did not read it the rest of the time on the journey to Terrabeth.

Five days later, the Daughters of Terrabeth could be seen in the far distance. From where the three men stood, the islands appeared like small hills protruding out of the sea. There were dozens of them, all placed in a way that caused them to form two lines, with a wide gap between the two rows of islands, creating a runway for ships coming from, and going to, the mainland. As the islands became closer, several docks could be seen coming off of the islands, with many songvissen calmly floating across the bay shores, spontaneously bellowing out their calls. Bushy palm trees littered the islands, causing the islands to appear like green mounds from afar. Some of the palms even grew beneath the seawaters near the island shores, and sprouted up above the water's surface.

Before the first two islands, at the entrance of the wide opening between the two lines of islands, were two massive stone pillars that came up from the ocean, each standing about thirty feet tall. The pillars were a pasty white color, each with a carving of a songvis, facing away from the islands, on each pillar. The songvissen on the pillars were sitting on top of an engraved pile of food, clothing, jewelry, currency coins, and weapons. The other three sides of the rectangular pillars had palm trees carved onto them, with the palm branches set on fire. Atop each of the two pillars was a long silver pole that had a long and thin sapphire-dyed streamer attached to it, showing the direction of the blowing wind.

Soon enough, the ship reached the first few islands, and Elijah and Jeremiah observed this new place from the ship. The happenings on the island continued as they sailed, ignoring the large ship. This area was a busy port for the mainland of Terrabeth, and so a ship coming through this area was nothing out of the ordinary for the natives.

Elijah looked over the edge of the ship to see young children splashing in the shallow waters near the shore, as songvissen lay across the shores, basking in the brightness of the sun that was right above them, lighting this noonday.

Jeremiah watched as he saw many men riding small paddleboats in the sea, pulling in nets filled with silver fish that were flapping back and forth, trying to escape, but without a hope for any of them. He noticed that although all the people had the same color hair and skin as Royce, most men were not as short as Royce was. Many of these people were not dressed in tunics like Royce, but were instead almost in rags that were dirty, and seemed to be worn out. Men that did wear tunics watched and spoke with each other, while the ones in dirtied clothing worked.

"Why have we not caught their attention?" Jeremiah asked,

confused at how the many people working around them, and even other ships sailing about, had ignored their arrival.

"There is nothing unusual about us," Royce explained smiling, as the ship's speed decreased, but still pushed on toward the mainland that was still too distant to be seen from where they stood. "The Daughters are a main port for our land, and even for the entire known world. Many ships come in and out of here, everyday, transporting different foods, items, and even animals, to sell and trade. Some of the hardest workers in our kingdom are here now, before your eyes. The men you see standing off to the side in finer clothing are from the mainland. It is their products that are sold and traded, and they are the ones who buy from other men. The other men you see in dirtier clothing work for them. They might not make as much money as the men in tunics, but it's enough for them to live off of."

Royce looked to his right to see familiar faces of men in fine sapphire colored tunics, having a conversation with each other. Before any of the men could take notice of Royce, he stepped away from the ship's edge.

"This day is getting hot," Royce said, walking toward the stairway. "I'm going downstairs to sit in the shade."

Royce was able to go down the stairs before the group of men could have seen him, and Elijah and Jeremiah were too visually engaged with their surroundings to notice Royce's real reason for leaving the deck.

"Had you ever even dreamed of anything like this before?" Elijah asked Jeremiah as they continued to look out at the new sights surrounding them.

"Never could I have imagined anything like this," Jeremiah said, resting his hands on the wooden rail on the front edge of the ship. "This is nothing like anything we have ever seen, and it's only the first of several lands we will get to encounter. I almost don't even want to try imaging what they would be like, as though I were to spoil the surprise of my eyes laying hold of them for the first time."

"The journal told me a bit about the rest of the world," Elijah spoke softly, even though Royce was already gone, and Elijah was alone with Jeremiah. "But I don't believe it goes into greater detail until later in the writings. While these exact things we see now didn't exist in the time this book was written, it at least talks about what these lands looked like long ago."

"Then maybe you should stop reading it," Jeremiah provoked. "You're the adventurous one, aren't you? Don't you want to be surprised when you discover these places for the first time?"

"I'm learning from the journal," Elijah responded, almost defensive.

"Is it aiding you in this journey?" Jeremiah questioned. "Besides the location of the weapons, what else in those accounts has brought you answers to questions in need of resolution? If anything, it's only caused us trouble."

"I was instructed to keep it safe," Elijah spoke back.

"And to keep it hidden," Jeremiah breathed. "You were to use its maps to get us to the items, not read it for enjoyment. Doing that has almost caused the journal to be exposed."

Elijah had no response to this.

"You cannot read it as frequently as you did when we first began this journey," Jeremiah ordered him. "When we were alone, the journal could be taken out and read as you wished. Now, being surrounded by other people, foreigners at that, having the journal out will only cause us trouble."

"You're right," Elijah said, spitefully agreeing with Jeremiah.

"I don't mean to discourage you," Jeremiah warmly said, putting his hand on Elijah's shoulder and gripping it gently, "but our travels have now become much more dangerous. We are in lands we have never been to, amongst people we don't know. We cannot take the risk of endangering ourselves, and falling off task. The journal is more powerful than any sword or bow our kingdom offers. We cannot cause it to fall back on us and bring harm upon our home."

Understanding his keeper's words, Elijah silently looked to Jeremiah, and nodded his head.

By early evening, they had finished passing by the final islands that were closest to the coast of Terrabeth. Two lines of palm trees that were growing out of the sea stretched across the gap in the sea between the last two islands, and the shores of the mainland. The branches of the palms were set afire, blazing constantly without burning the branches, because the branches had been dowsed in a special oil called Balm of Terrabeth, that, locally, came from underwater caves beneath the Daughters of Terrabeth.

These lines of burning palms served as a guide to the area of the coast where ships could dock, or, continue sailing on a river that flowed northward, out of the sea, and up through the land of Terrabeth. It ran all the way up to the castle of King Phillip, the king of Terrabeth. From the castle, the river then curved to the left, and ran back down to the sea, more or less running parallel with its first half. The entrance and exit to this river was practically side by side, but as it went up through the land, the two halves of the river ran as far apart as an hour's walk.

"That's the mainland," Royce told Elijah and Jeremiah as they walked up from the stairway, and saw the path they were on. "Do you know exactly where we must go?"

"No," Elijah said, not even realizing beforehand that he did not have an exact location of where to find the armor.

"Terrabeth is a huge continent," Royce told him. "Some of the other continents we will be going to after this are even larger. Do you really have no idea where this belt may be hidden?"

"I suppose not," Elijah said, realizing this journey would be much more difficult than he had anticipated, a sense of discouragement filling his veins.

"Either way," Royce said, attempting to lighten Elijah's burden, seeing that they were about to reach the shore area and begin their travels through Terrabeth's mainland, "it would be safer for us to not sail up the river."

"Why is that?" Jeremiah quickly asked. "What danger is on that path?"

"The river itself holds no threat," Royce spoke back, looking to the steady moving river in the distance. "The Royal River leads to the capital city of Terrabeth, and directly under the bridge entrance of the castle of our king. Once you have set sail onto it, you cannot leave its water, not even to dock, until you have reached the castle at the river's midway point. It runs about two days travel into the land, where the capital is, and then it takes just as long to ride it back down to this area."

"Would your king be able to help us?" Elijah quickly brainstormed. "Would he possibly know about the belt we are looking for?"

"I doubt it," Royce responded. "Your fairytales are unlike anything I've ever heard of. And still, in addition to the rules of riding that river, its passage is only meant for those who are going to visit the king. Visitors must offer their best gift of great worth, and value, to the him. If the king doesn't approve of the offering, the guest's ship, along with all the property within it, will become the king's. Anyone else aboard the ship will be seized, and forced into slavery."

"And what if he approves?" Elijah asked, noticing that the river ahead had no ships on it.

"Then you may continue on safely," Royce said, looking back to his sails that were still gathering the little wind that was blowing. "You can stay in the city, leaving your ship docked at the bridge, until you wish to leave. While sailing down river, you are not allowed to stop at any point. You must keep travelling until you have returned to the sea."

"Does the king usually accept the gifts offered to him?" Jeremiah wisely questioned.

"It depends on the king," Royce anxiously responded, turning his back toward the mainland.

Royce then went to pull down the worn sails of his ship, and the ship slowly came to a rest near one of the long stone docks that came up from the sea, allowing many ships to park. Two of Royce's songvissen gently nudged the ship into place, securely parking it at the dock.

The songvissen all pulled their heads out of the water and

watched as Royce and his two friends stood on the ship's side, ready to depart. From their mouths came a saddening song as one of them transported the three men from the ship to the stone dock.

"I'll return to you soon," Royce said as the songvis that had just transported him lowered its head down to where Royce stood, Royce's reflection showing on the side of the large gem on the songvis' forehead.

Royce put his hand over the smooth skin of the songvis and, for a brief moment, Royce rested his forehead against its massive head, showing his affection for the creature, wishing it farewell for the time being. After that, the three men began to walk down the dock, toward the sandy beach that was filled with many tents and wooden shops that formed a constantly busy market place.

By the time they reached the market place, the sun had set, and the three travelers found themselves amongst hundreds of other people who were of various skin colors, hair styles, sizes, and shapes.

"Stay near," Royce said, pulling the hood that was sewn onto his tunic over his head, concealing his face from easily being visible, as they walked into the market place. "This place is always filled with people, many from all over the world. Some are friendly, while others are not. Don't stray away. We must stay together."

The Courts of Phillip

Royce led Elijah and Jeremiah, pushing their way through the crowds of people that filled up the massive market place. Elijah could not help but stare, seeing various types of people with skin colors he had never seen before, and with hairstyles he had never witnessed. Even the shapes of their faces and bodies were new to him.

Straight rows of palm trees that extended about thirty feet directly up into the air were burning like the ones in the sea, keeping the sandy area well lit. Lined up with the palms were rows of tables and stands where merchants were selling goods that originated from different areas of the known world.

Elijah's eyes were drawn to a different sight every few seconds, taking in this new world he had been hidden away from his whole life. As he passed by a table of different cloths to his right, he brushed his hands against the rough hide of a large mammal he did not know of, and then following the hide came a finely woven blanket of velvet.

"Don't touch anything, Elijah," Jeremiah told him from his left side, pulling at his left arm.

"Could the belt be sold here somewhere?" Elijah asked Royce, catching up to him, and walking beside him.

"It's possible, but it would be difficult to find it here," Royce said as they walked by a small pen of goats that were crying out loudly, kicking at the hay beneath their jagged hooves. "This market place extends very far and wide from the shore, and business here never slows down. It would take at least a few days to go through all the merchants, asking for your belt."

Looking to the row of stands to his left, Jeremiah saw one that had all sorts of musical instruments made from brass and wood. Hanging from a pole at the stand were wooden flutes that were different lengths and colors. The sight of this reminded him of his brother, Micah.

"Two silver coins for a wooden flute!" the merchant selling the instruments yelled out at Jeremiah, noticing Jeremiah's fixation on the flutes. "They're carved from rare trees that grow violet leaves, which can only be found surrounding the waterfalls in Terrazain!"

"Terrazain doesn't even have waterfalls," Royce mumbled to Elijah. "He's just trying to make a sale."

Jeremiah quickly turned his head forward, away from the man

and his stand, as he continued to try to get Jeremiah's attention so to sell him a flute. His yells became faded amongst the many other voices as Jeremiah continued to walk away, trailing behind the other two travelers, the crowd of people surrounding them beginning to separate him from Elijah and Royce.

Jeremiah then quickly began to gently push through the crowd that formed between him and his companions, trying to catch up to where Royce and Elijah were walking ahead.

Suddenly, one of the men Jeremiah nudged in front of pushed Jeremiah, knocking him forward into other people, the group of them falling to the ground. The man who pushed him was much taller than Jeremiah, and was dressed in an expensive sapphire colored tunic.

"Watch yourself!" the man yelled at Jeremiah, as Jeremiah quickly got to his feet, turning to face the man as the crowd around them quickly disbursed, leaving a gap in the massive crowd of people. "How dare you push by me like that!"

Ready to fight, and drowned out by his pride, Jeremiah immediately drew his sword out, and random screams amongst the crowd could be heard. Royce turned around right away, as he and Elijah were pushed away from Jeremiah by the crowd that was rushing past them, the bystanders attempting to keep clear of the fight that was about to follow their panic.

"And now you threaten me with your sword," the man said,

pulling out two long and thin maces that were hanging over his hips. "How dare you threaten a member of the House of King Phillip in his home nation!"

Jeremiah stood silent, sword raised, as the man began to spin the two maces, one in each of his hands. Jeremiah had never seen weapons like the ones this man was wielding, so he cautiously observed their movements in the stranger's hands.

"Jeremiah!" Elijah yelled, pushing by the last few people, leading himself and Royce to rush into the open area with Jeremiah.

"Derrick!" Royce yelled, quickly standing between the two hot-headed men, pulling his hood back to clearly reveal his face to the tall man who had pushed Jeremiah.

"Royce?!" the man yelled back confused, stilling the spinning weapons in his hands.

"Yes, Derrick," Royce said, walking up to the man, "I've returned."

"With this short-tempered boy?" Derrick growled back, still angered by Jeremiah.

"They are from another land, Derrick," Royce explained, calming him down as Elijah and Jeremiah stood several feet behind him, Jeremiah's sword still held up. "They aren't accustomed to our lands. Please, forgive them."

"If you were any other man, your words wouldn't be enough," Derrick said, hooking his maces back onto his side, "but, because we are family, I will do as you ask of me."

"Family?" Elijah asked, putting his hand on Jeremiah's arm, applying pressure to lower his sword. "He said he was a member of the King's House. What does he mean by these things? Royce, are you a prince?"

"No," Royce breathed out heavily, turning back to his foreign friends. "Derrick is my brother, and he is a member of the House of King Phillip, but I am not."

"Then is your brother a prince?" Jeremiah asked confused, putting his sword back in its sheath.

"Not technically." Royce continued to clarify. "Let me explain. Most of the known world is politically broken up into six realms known as the Six Sects, informally known as the Terra Six. Each of these Sects is independently ruled and overseen by a single king, and each king has a single advisor, who gives him aid, and helps instruct him in making major decisions. Upon being declared the king's advisor, the advisor is made a member of the House of his king, and given the rights of the royal family."

"So you are the advisor to King Phillip?" Elijah asked, walking up to Derrick.

"No," Derrick explained even more. "Royce and mine's brother,

Darius, is the Advisor of Terrabeth. When our parents died, during a time of great plagues brought upon our land by war with an enemy nation, Darius begged the king to take us, his only brothers and his last living relatives, into the House of Phillip. King Phillip kindly allowed it. Though we don't bear the titles, we bear the rights of princes in this nation."

"With such privilege, why would you have ever left this land?" Jeremiah asked Royce confused.

"Derrick," Elijah quickly intervened, changing subjects, knowing how this was a sensitive subject for Royce, as Derrick began to fearlessly stare at Royce in response to Jeremiah's question, "perhaps you can help us."

"No," Royce gasped, grasping onto Elijah's shoulder, pulling him away from Derrick.

"Help you with what?" Derrick cunningly began to draw in Elijah's attention.

"It has nothing to do with you, Derrick," Royce said, as Jeremiah walked up beside him. "We are merely travelling."

"What nation are you from?" Derrick questioned the young Elijah who was still looking up to Derrick, whose straight and long blonde hair hung down to the end of the stubbly, narrow chin.

"They are from a neighboring continent," Royce answered for Elijah. "I met them, and have joined them into my travels. There is nothing more to this."

"Your travels have gone for years now, brother," Derrick said, walking up to Royce who was nearly half his height, bending over, and placing a hand on Royce's shoulder. "Darius and I have missed you in your absence! You must come to the castle, and visit for at least a day."

"We are busy on our travels," Royce argued. "We have no time for that."

"No time for you own family?" Derrick responded loudly, digging his fingertips into his brother's shoulder. "Actually, we have been waiting for your return."

"No, Derrick." Royce continued to deny the invitation. "I can't."

"We must be on our way," Elijah said, jumping into the conversation.

"Our king is very knowledgeable," Derrick said, turning his attention back to Elijah. "Whatever help you are in need of, I am sure he can offer proper aid."

Derrick then put his arm around Royce, and took him aside from where the other two men stood. Elijah and Jeremiah carefully watched as Derrick hunched over, and put his head besides Royce's, Derrick's thin red lips level with Royce's left ear.

"You can either be returned to Darius as a guest," Derrick

whispered softly, his voice only reaching as far as Royce's ear, "or, as a prisoner."

Royce paused, knowing the fate that was awaiting him at the castle. Derrick slowly stood back up, dusting the dirt off of his thick knees, as Royce turned back to his fellow travelers.

"I must go with him," Royce told the other two who were waiting.

"We will go with you," Elijah boldly stated.

"You must continue on your journey," Royce quickly said.

"We will," Elijah responded. "And we will continue it with you."

"We won't get far without you," Jeremiah added. "We will accompany you to the castle."

"Wonderful!" Derrick happily said as the area around them slowly became crowded, returning to normal. "My ship is docked by the entrance to the Royal River. Let's go now!"

"But we have nothing special to offer the king," Elijah said as Derrick began to walk away, causing the other three to follow behind him.

"My brother's presence will be just as worthy an offering as any precious stone would be," Derrick said loudly as the four walked through the heavily crowded area. "We have been waiting for his return for some time now."

The group of four men then walked back to the dock area, boarded Derrick's ship, and then sailed onto the Royal River, which would take them to the Courts of Phillip in a matter of two days.

Once on the river, the men did not speak with each other, and only went to bed, sleeping as the ship smoothly sailed over the deceitfully deep river. Derrick slept in his own private room on his ship, as did Royce. Elijah and Jeremiah shared a small guest room between the other two occupied rooms. Along with these four men on the ship were Derrick's crew of ten men who were steering the ship, and were there to guard Derrick, even though this was not a time of war for Terrabeth. The ten men stayed in a large open area at the bottom of the ship, and only came out when they were needed.

At dawn, Royce woke up, and went up to the dock, stepping back into the warm and humid air that left a thick blanket of fog rolling over the river.

"Don't tell me you're trying to run away again, are you?" Derrick's voice sounded from behind Royce, causing him to turn around and see his brother walking onto the deck of the ship, coming from the stairwell.

"I wouldn't abandon my friends, and leave them with you," Royce responded as Derrick walked up to him, forcing Royce to look up to his face.

"You've had that same level of loyalty in the past," his brother said back, turning away from him, and walking to the edge of the dock, watching the dense forest that surrounded the river slowly pass by them. "And yet, you've been nowhere to be found for a very long time now."

"I am not who I was before," Royce said forcefully, walking to his brother's side, gripping his own fists tightly as he approached him. "And I will never go back to those ways."

"You will do as I tell you to do," Derrick growled back at his younger brother, "or I will expose you for who you truly are."

Royce stood silent, fearful to say anything to provoke Derrick to act out on the actions he was threatening him with.

"That's what I thought," Derrick contently spoke. "Your two friends will be safe, along with your secrets, as long as you do as you are told. If you try to take actions against us, or thwart our plans, you will be exposed. You will officially lose your rights, your friends, and your life."

Royce's dirty nails dug into his sweaty palms as he gripped his hands even tighter, standing speechless at the threat given to him. After the last several years of Royce's past, his brothers now had the upper hand in a family controversy that had consumed their relationships.

For the rest of the day, Derrick remained alone in his private room, not interacting with the three travelers he had brought aboard.

The following afternoon, they reached the capital city. The three travelers watched together as the surrounding forest disappeared, and was replaced by a massive area filled with dome shaped buildings of grey stone. The city was in the shape of a half circle, with all its buildings and monuments facing a long castle of charcoal colored stone that took up the top second half of the circle shaped city. There was a gap in the land between the castle and the city, but a wide stone bridge connected the two, with the Royal River passing under this bridge.

The castle had no towers, and only stood about six stories high, having a flat rectangular shaped front side. Atop the center of the flat roof of the castle was a dome constructed of reflective silver glass that could not be seen through, and all along the roof were multiple silver poles that had sapphire colored banners flowing with the gusting wind that would suddenly come and go.

The land that the city was settled in was shaped like a bowl, with a high mountain range surrounding the backside of the castle, north of the capital city. At the center of this mountain range was a massive extinct volcano that had never, in Terrabeth's recorded history, shown signs of life.

As they continued to sail down the Royal River, they periodically passed by pillars that were similar to the ones they saw when they first entered the waters surrounding the Daughters of Terrabeth, but, instead of long flags on the top of the pillars, there stood sculptures of men.

"Who are those men?" Elijah asked Royce as they stood on the deck, pointing to one the sculptures they were passing by.

"Some are former kings," Royce explained. "Others are heroes from Terrabeth who have proven themselves worthy of remembrance through acts of valor, bravery, and wisdom."

As they drifted closer to the castle, Jeremiah noticed four statues of men placed on the top of the center of the castle roof, standing in front of the glass dome. The men were all standing at attention, overlooking the city.

"And them?" Jeremiah asked Royce, pointing to the four men.

"Those four are the founders of Terrabeth," Royce told him. "They were the cause for everything you see here. They brought law and unity to the people of this land, uniting them under one banner of ruling. Before their actions, this was a land of chaos, and disorder."

"So is Terrabeth the leader of the Six Sects?" Elijah asked, still uncertain about how the new world he had been thrust into worked.

"No," Royce informed him. "None of the Six Sects have authority over each other. Some have alliances with each other, but just as well some are enemies against each other. The Six Sects rule over most of the world, but there are still some continents and lands that are not under ruling of any of the Six Sects. Some of these other nations have governments, while the others live freely without authority over them. They have, for the most part, always been looked over by the Six Sects, passed off as primal, and uncivilized people groups."

"Do the Six Sects ever try to take control over those other nations?" Jeremiah asked.

"They did, generations ago, when the Six Sects first came into power," Royce spoke. "But the legal borders across the world that are established now have not been altered for nearly just as many generations."

"Will we get to see the Six Sects?" Elijah asked Royce, excited for the adventure ahead.

"If I remember correctly, we will see five of them," Royce smiled back to his friend, seeing how traveling across the world brought him joy. "But the sixth place we will be going to is a forgotten land, outside of the ruling of any of the Terra Six."

Derrick then walked out onto the deck of the ship as they neared the castle, causing the conversation between the three developing companions to end.

The river then began to curve to the left, bringing them under the large bridge they had seen from afar. Once under the bridge, the ship came to a halt in front of a wire gate that was extended across the river, blocking ships from freely passing. Scattered across the bottom of this bridge were many guards that were dressed in thick dark blue tunics, with shiny silver breastplates that had a songvis engraved onto the front side. Each guard had a silver helmet, with a lump on the helmet over their foreheads, resembling the forehead of a songvis.

"This way," Derrick told the three other men, walking to the right side of the ship, where the castle entrance could be viewed.

The section of the bridge to their right had a wide opening for river travelers to enter through, leaving their ships and possessions behind while they went to visit the king. This opening in the wall of the bridge was the beginning of a long and wide walkway that led to the Courts of Phillip, the throne room of the king.

Four guards that were standing at the walkway entrance slid out, toward the ship, a long metal beam that was about three feet wide. The beam reached out through the air, and connected to Derrick's ship, giving the men aboard the ship the ability to walk from their ship, to the entrance in the bridge. The four men walked across it, being led by Derrick, and entered onto the stone walkway.

"Sir," a guard who held a metal spear said, approaching Derrick. "Are these your guests?"

"Yes," Derrick spoke, walking past the guard, with the other three men trailing behind him.

The sight of Royce quickly caught the attention of the guard, and he silently watched as the four men went down the walkway. As the four of them continued, the hallway turned into a wide staircase, leading them up to the throne room. After reaching the fortieth step, the staircase ended, and the group found themselves standing in the middle of the Courts of Phillip.

The room was at the center of the castle, and was as tall as the castle itself. Across the walls of the room were large silver jars filled with the same oil used on the palm trees in the market place they had been at days before. The tops of the jars were set on fire, leaving the room to be lit continuously this way. In addition to this, the silver glass dome on the top of the castle served as a sunroof to this room, adding to the illumination.

Scattered along the walls, and surrounding the jars, silently sat women and children. They were all dressed in the same thin white robes, and had the hair on their heads shaved off. Circles of black ink had been painted around their eyes, and a black circle was painted on each of their foreheads. Many of them had necks that were two to three times the length of a normal person, while others were wearing silver rings around their necks that were forcing their necks to grow longer. It was obvious they were all underfed, because each one was very thin, with their cheekbones bulging outward due to their caved in cheeks. The very life of these individuals seemed to have been drained from them because not one of them showed any expression.

At the head of the room was a platform, elevated by six steps, where a large throne of gold rested. To the right hand of the throne was a silver throne that was very similar to the golden one, the only notable difference being that it was much smaller. To the left hand side of the golden throne was a thin blue stool. On the golden throne sat King Phillip, on the silver one sat his advisor, Darius, and on the blue stool silently sat the king's daughter, Princess Beth.

Behind that platform, along the wall, was a small garden of bushy palm trees that had grown to about half the height of the wall of the throne room. Above the palm trees, carved out of the stone wall, was a large hole.

"Darius!" King Phillip loudly said, his voice echoing through the room. "Could this be? Your brother has returned?"

The four men quickly came to the foot of the steps of the platform to honorably bow before the king, with Elijah and Jeremiah following Royce and Derrick's actions seconds after, trying to seem as though they knew how to carry themselves in this setting.

Darius, with hair just like his brothers', clothed in heavy sapphire colored robes, leaned forward in his seat, looking down to the group who were still bowing. Elijah looked up, and caught sight of Darius, his eyes piercing into Elijah's gaze, like a hook into the mouth of a fish.

"Stand," King Phillip ordered the four of them, as his daughter's face continued to stare forward, but with her slightly slanted eyes looking down to the men.

The king's hair was wavy, reaching down to his shoulders,

and was the color of yellow hay, and grey rain clouds. Wrinkles were scratched across his face, and he was dressed in a thick layer of sapphire colored robes, stitched with golden thread, with a large golden crown sitting on his oval shaped head. The front of the crown had a large sapphire stone implanted on it.

His daughter was draped in deep blue colored silk that poured down her body, and onto the marble ground of the platform beneath her stool. Her hair was so blonde it was nearly white, and was all folded upward, decorated in silver lacing that served as a type of tiara, with a clear stone from a songvis attached to the front of it, leaving it to rest on her forehead. Like the slaves and songvis alike, black paint circled around her eyes, causing the white of her eyes to shine even brighter, followed by intensely deep grey eyes. Her hands, slightly tanned from her time spent in the palace's outdoor garden, remained folded on her lap, and her face never moved in another direction other than forward while she sat perched on her stool.

"Royce, explain yourself," the king commanded, looking to Royce, as the four men stood to their feet. "You have been missing for years now. You informed no one of your departure, and left us with no idea as to where you were going."

"I departed to sail the seas," Royce said loudly so that the king could hear, but respectfully so to not anger him. "The winds took me far from here, and only recently seemed to have favored me enough to return me home."

Darius stood from his throne, and walked down to where Royce stood, Beth's raging stare devouring their presence.

"Brother," Darius said with relief, bending over to hug Royce, because Darius was even taller than Derrick, "we have missed you."

"And you others," the king said, looking to Elijah and Jeremiah, "who are you?"

"They are my friends," Royce said, breaking away from the hug he was barely giving effort toward. "I found them while on my journeys. They are foreigners from another land."

"What land?" the king enquired. "Are you from one of the Six Sects?"

"We are from the Kingdom of Abel," Elijah responded to the king.

"Kingdom of Abel?" the king spoke confused. "I have never heard of that place. Which continent is your kingdom located?"

"It's not on a known continent," Royce interjected. "I found them on a land that is not on any map I have ever seen."

"You two foreigners may walk onto my platform," the king kindly told Elijah and Jeremiah as Darius walked back onto the platform, and returned to his seat.

Elijah and Jeremiah quickly walked up the steps as King

Phillip stood up from his throne, and motioned his open hands downward to the floor of the platform. Once on the platform, the two foreigners looked to the marble floor beneath them, seeing a map of the world that was just like the map on the deck of Royce's ship. The seas were colored white, and the lands were all black, except for the lands of Terrabeth, which were filled in with sapphire.

"Show me," King Phillip again commanded. "Where is your land?"

Without saying a word, Elijah looked to the wide-open ocean of white beneath the king, and pointed at its center, which was under the king's throne.

"There," Elijah said softly to the king as Darius slyly watched from his seat while his two brothers remained standing at the base of the platform.

The king had no response to this. His grey eyes blankly stared at the white sea beneath his throne, mesmerized at the spot where Elijah pointed to.

"Leave my platform," he quietly said to them, and they rejoined Royce right away.

Without another word, the king took his seat on his throne, and loud stomping could be heard coming from the opposite side of the wall behind the palm trees. From the hole above the palms popped out the head of a songvis that had its head decorated in gold-chained jewelry, a portion of its long neck following behind it as its head slithered into the throne room. Without singing a note, the songvis looked down to Elijah.

The slaves all along the walls quickly bowed down, placing the dried black paint on their foreheads against the cold ground beneath them. Without a word, Beth slid off of her stool, her hands still folded across her lap, and her face remaining emotionless.

Elijah looked up to the songvis, and their sights became caught up in each other's, as though the songvis was looking deep into Elijah's heart, and Elijah was whispering to it every secret he ever had. The very breath in Elijah's lungs seemed to be sucked away, and the beating of his heart was made still.

The clear stones on the songvis' neck began to glow up toward its mouth, and once all the stones had lit up, the songvis opened its mouth, releasing a towering melody that permeated the humid air. Unlike any other songvis, the large stone on its forehead began to glow a brilliant shade of colors that bounced forth across the color spectrum.

Jeremiah turned to the princess to see the large stone on her forehead glowing in a similar way to the royal songvis'. This was an excuse for Jeremiah to look at the beautiful princess. While he did this, Elijah noticed Jeremiah's eyes fixed on her in a way that was not due to the stone hanging over her forehead.

After about fifteen seconds of singing, the songvis became

silent, yet the large stone on its forehead continued to glow.

"Travelers from distant shores," Beth began to sing, repeating the same notes the songvis had just sung, "shores long since hidden away. Into the dark you have been sent, to find a light that wakes the day."

At the end of Beth's words, the songvis sang again for about the same length of time it had first sung for. Beth's face was unmoved, continuing to shed no insight into her thoughts, even as she sang the interpretation of the beast's melody.

"Six stars they shine across this earth," Beth's soothing voice continued to flow. "Together they chase the moon away. Together these six will bring the birth, of a hope that for a generation will stay."

The songvis began again, leaving its listeners hungry for Beth to explain its mysteries in a language they could comprehend.

"Make haste, and be quick, on your way you must go," Beth sang, her voice suddenly becoming shaky, her eyes widening and watering as she blankly stared forward. "Or your land will be drenched, bathed in shadow, before you return, to revive sleeping hope. Make haste, and be quick, on your way you must go."

At her final note, two tears tumbled down her high cheek bones, her hands quickly reaching to her face to wipe them away, lightly smearing the black paint around her eyes. The stones across the songvis, and the stone on Beth's forehead dimmed, losing their light, and silence fell upon the room. Just as smoothly as the royal songvis had slid its head into the Courts of Phillip, it slid its head back out, returning to its home in the royal garden, which was behind this wall.

"Is it the Six Sects you are in need of aid from?" Darius questioned the two foreigners as the songvis loudly stomped away from the wall. "Are we the six stars?"

"No," Jeremiah answered, making sure to speak before Elijah did, so that no especially secretive information could be given. "We are looking for an armor that we believed was forged in our land."

Beth took a deep breath, and sat back upon her stool. As she did this, the slaves along the wall sat up from their bowing positions.

"How could armor from your nation be in foreign lands?" Darius argued, prying Jeremiah for more answers. "Your home is unknown to the rest of the world."

"I do not know," Jeremiah said, hesitating to speak words before he thought out whole sentences in his head. "But, I believe one article of the armor that we are looking for is in Terrabeth."

Elijah turned his gaze toward Royce, noticing that Royce was looking to Beth, his eyes almost calling out to draw her attention, and obtain her sight.

"And what is this article, young man?" Darius asked,

cornering Jeremiah into giving a definite fact of their travel plans.

"A belt," Jeremiah spoke softly.

"A belt?!" Phillip nearly shouted, breaking into the conversation. "Surely you are not talking about Terrabeth's Bane?"

"They do," Beth quietly whispered to her father, lowering her head, looking to the marble floor beneath her.

"I don't know what you are speaking of," Jeremiah responded, confused at what was being talked about.

"How can you look for something, yet claim to know nothing of it?" Darius spoke, regaining the conversation from the king, trying to trap Jeremiah with his words. "Why would you look for such a cursed thing? And you said it is from your native land. Was it some sort of failed plot to overthrow our four founders?"

"You have our word," Elijah interrupted, "we know nothing of a cursed belt."

"What was a curse to us," Beth softly spoke to her father, still looking to the marble ground, "will be a blessing to them."

Her shivering eyes looked to Elijah, foreseeing the fate of his homeland in all of this, her vision aided by the insight given through the songvis' melody. This stirring of emotions had caused her to lose her perfect composure, a sight never seen before on this platform.

"I will show them the way," Beth once more spoke out of

turn, another occurrence that had never taken place before this day.

"I will not risk my daughter's safety for such a foolish venture," the king huffed back at Beth.

"Please, your majesty," Elijah begged the king. "Please, if not by her aid, then just tell us the way, and we will go ourselves."

"Slaves!" Darius announced, standing to his feet, stretching his arms outward. "Leave now!"

The groups of slaves quickly stood, and raced out of the room, scurrying away like mice, leaving through the stairway that the men had entered through.

"My king," Darius bent over and whispered into Phillip's ear. "Perhaps they can aid us in multiple ways if we send them on their way."

"Go on," the king responded to Darius as Beth returned to her stoic pose.

"You will be shown the way, foreigners," Darius loudly said to the men below him, taking steps forward on the platform. "Royce will be your guide. We will give you access to what you are looking for, so long as you agree to fulfill a duty for us."

"What is the duty you require of us?" Jeremiah slyly questioned, attempting to combat Darius' manipulative scheming.

"Once you agree, I will tell you," Darius trapped Jeremiah.

"We will not agree to an unknown contract," Jeremiah argued as Darius returned to his seat.

"Very well, then," Darius chuckled, placing his hands together, his fingers tangling with one another. "Then we will not share its location with you."

"Please, do not do this to us," Elijah spoke frantically.

"You are doing this to yourselves," Darius replied. "It's not my kingdom that's in need of rescuing. If you truly do need to be as quickly on your way as possible, then you must agree immediately, before my mind is changed."

"Darius, please," Royce desperately said to his brother.

"Silence, Royce!" Darius yelled, pointing his hand at his youngest brother. "Until their decision is made, you will not speak, or you will be bound in chains! Perhaps then you will not go missing for years."

Derrick chuckled from behind Royce as Royce's ears began to burn, turning blood red as he fumed with anger.

"With every second you ponder, danger draws closer to your home," Darius continued on toward Elijah and Jeremiah. "They are in desperate need of your return, while you stand here in the comfort of this palace."

"Yes," Elijah spat out. "Yes, we agree."

"Just as I thought," Darius said, a devious grin slowly lifting his cheeks.

"What have we agreed to?" Jeremiah asked the advisor, knowing if Elijah had not caved in to Darius' terms, he himself would have.

"Once you have returned, you are to deliver a present to the king of Terrashin," Darius explained from his throne.

"What is the present?" Elijah asked Darius almost happily, realizing this was helping their travels, because Terrashin was their next scheduled stop after Terrabeth.

"An egg birthed by the royal songvis," Darius said, causing Royce's eyes to widen. "It will be a sign of our permanent peace and alliance with Terrashin. No greater gift could ever be given from all of Terrabeth."

"So how do we reach the belt?" Jeremiah quickly asked, trying to stay on task with retrieving the armor. "Where is it?"

"The history of the belt is a secret passed down from our four founders, only being shared with those of royal blood, and the advisors," Darius explained on behalf of the king who silently watched the events play out. "The belt was first found beside the sleeping volcano that stands behind this city, during the time when Terrabeth was first established. Its beauty and quality drew men to attempt to wear it, but all who wore it were immediately struck with deathly plagues never before seen, and some even died moments after wearing the belt. Even touching it brought sickness to many men. Attempts to destroy the belt by sword and flame did nothing. Because it was seen as a threat to the safety of our people, the four founders of Terrabeth ordered that the belt be taken away to the Northern Fire Pits, where no man could reach it. It was tossed into the widest fire pit, at the center of all the other pits, sinking to its bottom. That is where you will find the belt you are looking for. Royce will take you there."

"But how are we to retrieve it from the fire pit?" Jeremiah asked, angered by the complicated conditions of the journey.

"Royce will help you figure this out," Darius responded.

"Father," Beth spoke, breaking her composure for a final time, leaving her stool and falling to her knees before the king, frailly looking up to him, "please allow me to help them retrieve the belt. They will not be able to complete this task without me. Their nation is in need of our aid."

"It is a dangerous trek, Beth," Phillip replied. "You are the only other member of my bloodline. I cannot lose you."

"Please, allow me to go," Beth pleaded with her father.

"My king," Darius slithered in. "You should allow her to go. This will shorten the length of their quest to get the belt, causing our present to reach Terrashin much quicker."

A brief pause fell over the king as he looked down to his daughter beneath him, his compassionate gaze overcome by duty for his kingdom's prosperity.

"You may go," Phillip said, placing his hand on his daughter's cheek.

"Thank you, father," Beth gladly said, holding her father's hand, and kissing the back of it, while Darius sunk deep into his seat.

"It is night time now," King Phillip said to the travelers beneath him, while his daughter remained beside him. "You may rest in my palace for the night, and be on your way in the morning. The way to the Northern Fire Pits is not an easy one; you will need to be well rested. I will see to it that you will be sent with everything you need for your travels to and from the fire pits. You two foreigners will join us for dinner tonight, and then you will be taken to your bedrooms to sleep until morning."

Northern Fire Pits

"Where have you been all these years, Royce?" Beth angrily whispered to Royce as they stood in an empty hallway of the castle, far from any other listening ears than their own.

"Beth," Royce swiftly whispered back to the emotion struck princess, "I didn't have a choice."

"You left me with him," she said, her breaths shallow as her heartbeat increased while she fought back tears of frustration.

"It was the safest thing I could have done for you," he said back, trying to make amends for his absence.

"To leave me where your wretched brother, Darius, could continue to persuade my father to take my hand in marriage?" Beth hissed back.

"Five years, and he still hasn't been able to do that," Royce reminded Beth, gently taking hold of her hand.

"Five years, Royce," Beth cut in, pulling her hand away from him. "It has been five years since you vanished, without so much as a notice that you were leaving Terrabeth, and out of everyone here, you didn't even tell me goodbye."

"I'm sorry, Beth," Royce said, the weight of his decision to leave pressing down on him. "Darius' plots had evolved into something much greater than you or I could imagine. He had dragged me into it all. If I had stayed, I would have been forced to join his scheming, or framed and thrown into prison if I tried to resist. I left as secretly as I could so to successfully find refuge, anywhere away from home. Had I not left as quiet and swiftly, he would have had me captured. It wasn't until I met these friends of mine that I ever thought I would be back here."

"So you would have never come back for me?" Beth spoke, taking a deep breath.

"The sight of my demise would have done you more harm than for me to just disappear," Royce retorted. "And besides that, it's only been five years."

"Well," Beth began to speak, attempting to level out her emotions, "in those five years, Darius has taken more control than any advisor ever has before. My father rarely seems to even think for himself anymore. It's as though Darius is the king, and my father is his puppet; a spokesperson to carry out his will."

"My brother is capable of far worse things," Royce said, hesitating to say what he fully knew.

"What is he planning?" Beth questioned.

"I can't tell you," Royce slowly said, trying to figure out the right way to explain to Beth. "I just need you to trust me like you used to."

"That trust has left my heart," Beth said after a pause of silence. "Every night, for a year, I fell asleep at my window, watching the Royal River to see your boat return. But one year turned to two, two to three, until time passed to where we are now standing here, you with your secrets, and myself still alone."

"Beth," Royce said, putting his hand to hers again, his calloused hands folding over her smooth fingers, "I didn't mean to hurt you. I'm sorry."

Her eyes then looked down to see his hand over her own, and past emotions she had stored away years ago began to fight back for dominance, rushing over her like a flood.

"It's too late, Royce," Beth bitterly said, pulling her hand away from her lost love.

"Everything I ever did was out of my love for you," Royce firmly told her. "It was to protect you."

Without a response, Beth turned away, and began to walk down the hall, with the sound of her elegant blue gown dragging behind her echoing in the long stone hallway as Royce watched her leave him. His shoulders sunk low, and his head tilted downward, his eyes now catching a glimpse of his worn leather boots that had drawn him too far to return back to where he first came from. His heart seemed to drop down to the lowest part of his gut and for that moment, hopelessness triumphed over his drive to win her back.

That night, the whole group was seated for dinner at Phillip's table in the royal dining arena. The meal, which consisted of choice fruits and vegetables that were native to Terrabeth, was eaten in total silence, as was tradition for the people of this nation.

At the end of the meal, Royce took Elijah and Jeremiah up to a guest room where they would be staying for the night. Once they arrived there, Elijah and Jeremiah lay on their own beds, ready to sleep, but Royce left the room, saying he had grown thirsty, and went out to retrieve a glass of water.

"So this is how it is to be a prince?" Jeremiah said after taking a deep breath, resting in the large room of the palace, engulfed in comfort by his surroundings.

"In privilege, I suppose," Elijah grievously told him, "but not in responsibility."

A brief silence fell over them as they waited for Royce to return.

"What if it's not the belt we're looking for?" Elijah asked Jeremiah, drastically changing the subject, as they both laid on their backs, looking up to the stone ceiling above them, the bright moonlight shining into the room through the four open windows to their right.

"I can't imagine that being the case," Jeremiah responded, one of his hands placed under his head.

"They make it seem like such a horrid thing," Elijah said, his hands folded across his chest, as he laid in the bed that was next to Jeremiah, with two more beds after his own to his right. "Like it's an instrument of death, when we are looking for a precious piece of heaven."

"What was a curse to them," Jeremiah said, repeating the words of Beth, a slight grin forming on his face, causing his right dimple to crater in, "will be a blessing to us."

"Don't think I didn't take notice of your attention earlier," Elijah chuckled, turning onto his left side, facing Jeremiah, catching a glimpse of his smile. "You weren't just looking to the princess because she had something to say."

"I don't know what you're talking about," Jeremiah quickly denied, reforming his lips out of the arch they were in as Elijah sat up in his bed, facing Jeremiah.

"Why ponder the lifestyle of a prince, when you really want to be a king?" Elijah laughed, causing Jeremiah to grab the pillow that was underneath his head.

Jeremiah threw the pillow at Elijah with all his might, embarrassed by Elijah's comment, but Elijah dodged it, causing it to fly across the room, weightlessly crashing into the wall that had the open windows.

"Look what you've made me do, Elijah," Jeremiah said, as Elijah laughed. "Go get my pillow!"

"Fine," Elijah finished laughing, walking to pick up the pillow that had landed on the floor beneath one of the windows.

Once he reached the pillow, he knelt to picked it up. As soon as he rose back up, he looked out the window he stood in front of, and noticed two men speaking to each other far away in the garden area outside. It seemed to be a heated argument, because both men's arms were motioning around violently. As Elijah squinted his eyes, he could make out the two men: Royce and Darius.

"What do you see?" Jeremiah asked Elijah, noticing he was staring out the window.

Suddenly, Royce turned around, and stomped away from Darius. Elijah quickly backed away from the window, and returned to his bed, tossing Jeremiah's pillow back to him.

"Royce and Darius were outside talking with each other," Elijah explained, settling back in his bed. "It looked as though they were arguing."

"Could you hear them?" Jeremiah asked, returning the pillow to its place underneath his head.

"No," Elijah answered.

Several moments passed by as the two lay quietly, until the bedroom door opened, and Royce walked in, shutting the door behind him.

"Where is your glass of water?" Jeremiah questioned Royce as he walked up to the open bed furthest away from where Elijah was resting.

"Glass of water?" Royce responded, giving him time to think up an excuse. "I drank it, and left the empty glass elsewhere."

With that, no more words were exchanged for the night, and the three of them laid in silence. Elijah slept well that night, while Jeremiah and Royce slept little due to their own separate reasons.

The following morning, Elijah, Jeremiah, Royce, and Beth, set out on sturdy horses from the king's personal stable. The horses were abnormally tall, with thin legs that were purely muscle, enabling them to easily pass through narrow pathways along the rocky and mountainous treks ahead. Despite their disproportional bodies, they had perfect balance, with sharp hooves that stabbed into the ground like iron nails pounded into wooden planks. Their wide bodies were covered in black hair, with short dark blue manes that only grew about two inches long. Beth's horse had grey speckles sprinkled across the fur of its long snout.

The four travelers also each carried their own bag of food and water for the journey to and from the Northern Fire Pits. Elijah's bag also contained the journal he had failed to read for a time now.

As the middle of their first day of traveling came, they reached the top area of the mountain range that overlooked the capital city from the north. At the highest point of the area they were crossing, to the eastern side of the base of the volcano that still went higher, the four of them took a short pause for their horses to rest.

"Look at that," Jeremiah said, sliding off of his horse, walking toward the edge of the plateau they had reached, overlooking the capital city.

From this height, the glass dome tops of the houses, the dome on the palace roof, and the Royal River, were all brightly reflecting the sun's beams like mirrors, as the sun hung directly over the city. From this spot, the entire capital city looked like a massive white pearl radiantly shining. Had the travelers been closer to the city, their eyes may have been blinded.

"At midday, from afar, the city almost shines as bright as the sun itself," Royce said, walking up beside Jeremiah, followed by Elijah.

"It almost hurts to look at it," Elijah said, squinting his eyes, looking toward the city.

Beth stood beside her horse, silently caressing its thick neck, the breaths of the horse vibrating her hands. Though Beth was not wearing her royal gown, she still had her tiara type covering over her hair, with a thin blue hood over her head as well, and, as she always had no matter the time of day, the black paint around her eyes.

Elijah knelt down, picked up a small rough rock that was mixed into the sandy dirt beside his feet, and threw it off the mountain, watching it fall back into the forest they had traveled through in the first half of their hike up the mountain, miles below them.

"I bet I could throw it further," Royce said, digging around in the dirt for a rock to throw.

As Elijah and Royce threw rocks off the edge of the plateau, Jeremiah slid back, away from the edge, and walked toward Beth who was still beside her horse, watching Royce.

"Is he yours?" Jeremiah asked Beth, reaching her.

"Excuse me?" Beth quickly responded, breaking her stare from Royce to look at Jeremiah, her ears and cheeks turning pale red, placing her arms at her side.

"Is he yours?" Jeremiah said, Beth's face cringing in shock and confusion at Jeremiah's seemingly bold statement. "The horse, is he yours? You seem to have an attachment to him."

"Oh," Beth breathed out, relieved that she had misunderstood Jeremiah. "No. I have rarely ever left the palace walls. I've never needed my own horse, though I was trained to ride as a child. But, I do have an appreciation for them."

"They are different from the ones we have back home," Jeremiah began a casual conversation with Beth, as she began to pet the left side of the horse's neck. "They are much more slim and shorter where I come from."

"Ours are mountainous," Beth explained to Jeremiah, who had given her his full attention. "They are able to travel across rough terrain, like the kind that lies ahead on our journey north."

"Their colors are different as well," Jeremiah said, beginning to pet the right side of the horse's neck. "They're very unique and beautiful, but it seems most of the sights we have seen here in Terrabeth have been very beautiful so far."

Just as he said that, Royce turned around to see Jeremiah talking with Beth, the two of them petting the horse together.

"That's enough time for them to rest," Royce blurted out, interrupting their conversation, walking back toward the horses, where Jeremiah and Beth stood. "We have a long way ahead of us still. We must be on our way."

Elijah wiped his dusty hands across his sides, and returned to his horse. By the time he climbed back onto his horse, the other three had already mounted their horses, and were waiting for Elijah.

Again, Royce led the way, followed by Beth and Elijah who were riding beside each other, with Jeremiah trailing behind them. They were now beginning their trek down the backside of the mountain, continuing northward, in the direction they would be going in for the next several days.

"How do you do it?" Elijah asked Beth as they rode beside each other, the path up ahead of them soon to become narrow. "How can you understand what they are singing?"

"This stone over my head belonged to the first royal songvis," Beth explained. "When she died, her forehead's stone was carved to the size it is now, and given to the oldest princess of the third king of Terrabeth. The next songvis that replaced the deceased one was able to sing, and communicate a message by means of the stone. The wearer can interpret the song of the songvis, if the songvis chooses to share its message."

"Of all the songvis I have recently seen, none have had the stone on their foreheads glow," Elijah shared with the princess.

"It only glows when it is sharing a message with someone," Beth informed him. "And only daughters of Terrabethian kings have ever been able to hear their messages. Really, I've always been able to understand their songs. But, when I wear this stone, I can most accurately repeat the songs with human words. Without the stone, it's more so the feeling behind their song."

"So no other people have interpreted their songs before?" Elijah asked Beth, who was looking forward as they spoke.

"No," Beth responded, "not even our own kings."

At that point, the pathway narrowed, forcing the group to travel in a straight line down the mountain, cutting Elijah and Beth's conversation short.

Over the next five days, the group continued on their march northward, passing through forest after forest, taking few breaks, and camping at sunset each evening. By the fifth day, the air had become noticeably warmer, and much thinner. The terrain they were crossing now became a dry rocky range of hills, with little to no plant life around them. The skies dangled a thin sheet of grey clouds, the clouds seeming to be at an arm's reach above the travelers as they began reaching higher altitude. The stench of smoke began to slowly creep into their nostrils as they drew closer to their destination, a breeze blowing toward them from the north, carrying the smell.

"Each one of you has a scarf in your supply sack," Royce called out to the other three trailing behind him as he pulled a long light grey scarf that was especially thick, from his own pack of supplies. "Wrap it over your nose and mouth for protection. They are woven from the hair of beasts that live along the Frozen Crest in Terrashin. Their hair is thick enough to keep the smoke from getting to your mouth, but at the same time will allow you to breathe what little oxygen this place provides. The smoke from the Northern Fire Pits can be like poison in the lungs of man. Usually, you don't need covering until you actually reach the foot of the fire pits, but the wind is carrying the smoke toward us."

"Does that mean we are close?" Jeremiah asked Royce as they all wrapped the scarves around the bottom half of their heads.

"We are still about two days away from them," Royce shouted, his mouth covered by the scarf. "The wind is just not in our favor."

"They know we are coming," Beth whispered to herself beneath her scarf, looking forward to the end of the incline they were reaching the top of.

Moments later, once they had reached the peak of the incline, they were standing on high ground that overlooked a dry valley area that stretched northward for the rest of their travel, and after it, in the far distance, they could see a massive black mountain range, an orange aurora hauntingly radiating off the top of the mountains, with flowing rivers of completely black smoke pouring upward from the glowing, spilling into the mess of clouds above the mountains. The travelers could see the smoke intertwined with the clouds, coming in their direction, riding on the wind.

"There is said to be caverns throughout the valley ahead," Royce spoke out as they began to ride down from the high point, still moving northward. "We can find some to camp in during the nights that come before we reach the foot of the fire pits."

"Have you been here before?" Elijah called out to Royce, his voice muffled by the scarf over his mouth.

"No," Royce yelled back. "Very few people alive today have ever come to the fire pits, or the area near it. It's very unsafe."

"Because of the smoke?" Elijah asked, sweat gathering over his forehead.

"And the natives," Royce quietly said, his words unheard by the other three, then kicking his horse to move more quickly, getting far ahead of Elijah before Elijah could ask any more questions.

Once the sun began to lower itself in the sky, Royce began to scout through the rough terrain filled with boulders, looking for an entrance into any sort of hole or cavern where they could sleep in for the night.

Soon after, Royce found a narrow opening between a pile of rocks, which led down into the earth, guiding them to a small cave. Because it was pitch black in the cave, Royce, on foot, slowly walked into it, while the other three travelers, and the horses, waited for his command at the entrance of the cave, in the failing light of day that was barely visible in the open skies far behind them in their travels.

Shuffling his feet, Royce explored the cavern, his hands holding onto the side of the jagged stony wall. He stopped in his tracks, and removed the scarf from his face. A familiar scent of Terrabeth's oil for burning began to pet his sense of smell.

"Hello?" Royce called out into the cave, his voice echoing as it raced away into the endless abyss.

No response or sound followed.

Elijah, sliding off of his horse, pulled from his supply bag the stones they had brought with him from home, and began to strike them together, causing sparks to flash with every hit.

Slowly, he walked into the darkness where Royce stood ahead, slamming the rocks against each other with each step forward he took, his path being lit with every strike, enough for Royce to see from where he was now watching Elijah, but not enough for Elijah to see where he was going.

"Elijah!" Royce called to him. "Be careful! I smell oil in here!"

"Elijah!" Jeremiah yelled, slowly walking into the cave. "Get back over here!"

Hearing Jeremiah's voice, Elijah turned back to look at the tunnel he was walking through, the light at its entrance broken by a silhouette of Jeremiah. As he did, he took one last step forward, his boot falling onto a large wet stone, causing him to slip, and fall to the ground, landing a couple feet away from the stone he had stepped on. As he fell, the stones in his hands were tossed up into the air. Blinded by the darkness around Elijah, the others could not see what had just happened.

One of the two rocks quickly came back down to the ground, landing in the sandy earth several feet behind Elijah. The other, with precise aim, crashed into the wet stone Elijah had just slipped on, scratching at its surface. Immediately, the wet stone became engulfed in fire.

"Elijah!" Jeremiah yelled, running into the lit tunnel.

"What has happened?" Elijah questioned, confused, as Jeremiah and Royce both reached him.

The three looked around the tunnel, seeing small puddles of the bronze colored oil, with some rocks oozing the oil from their surface.

"There is more oil here than in any other area of Terrabeth," Royce said as Beth walked into the tunnel, leading the four horses behind her, two by two. "The Northern Fire Pits are giant risen pits of oil, burning continuously, never to burn out. The pits let out underground streams of oil that branch out beneath the valley surrounding them."

Jeremiah helped Elijah get back on his feet as Beth reached the area where they were standing, which, though was still somewhat narrow, had widened since the beginning of the tunnel, giving plenty of room to walk by the burning stone which was to the left side of the tunnel.

"It seems as though your stone was guided," Beth spoke to Elijah, the crackling of the flame echoing in the tunnel, as Elijah retrieved his two stones from the ground.

"I think it was," Elijah responded, perplexing Beth.

"Did you mean to strike that stone, and set it ablaze?" Beth interrogated Elijah as the group all began to walk further into the tunnel.

"No," Elijah answered. "It was completely dark, how could I have known it was there?"

"Exactly." Beth debated with the young prince who was about four years younger than her. "Then how could your stone have been guided? It only struck the rock by chance."

"Something greater than me must have guided it," Elijah shared.

"This makes no sense," Beth argued as they walked into a wide opening, ending their walk through the tunnel.

"It will soon," Elijah spoke, ending the conversation with Beth, walking away from her as she led the horses to one end of the massive cavern they had entered.

The fire from the tunnel gave little light to this cavern, but enough for Elijah to find a few puddles of oil. He set fire to them with his two stones, and brought illumination to the whole cavern. Oil slowly dripped down the cavern's walls, shimmering in the light of the fires Elijah had started.

"The air is safe to breathe here," Royce said, giving permission to the others to remove their face coverings, "but, we will most likely have to wear them again once we leave in the morning."

The four then ate together, in silence, in respect of Beth's tradition. Royce shared the same background, but was not one to care for abiding by customs.

Once they finished their small meals, the four sat around, waiting to become sleepy.

"So how were you chosen?" Beth asked both Elijah and Jeremiah, sitting across from them, with Royce sitting to her far left. "How were you picked to go on the journey you are on?"

"Well," Elijah began to ponder, "I suppose we volunteered to do this."

"Did no one else volunteer?" Beth continued to ask, trying to discover more about these two foreigners.

"Nobody else was offered the opportunity," Jeremiah responded.

"So then you were more so chosen for this task it seems," Beth said back to him.

"We were accepted to make this journey," Elijah interjected, accidently cutting off Jeremiah who desperately wanted to chat with Beth. "But, I believe more so we were chosen by a force greater than any man."

"Again, with your confusing speech?" Beth groaned, remembering Elijah's comment about the stone striking the rock earlier. "This makes no sense."

"They believe differently than us, Beth," Royce interrupted from where he sat, hunched over on his side. "Their people hear a voice from the sky, who they believe created the world around them. They say this voice is in control of everything, too."

"Silliness," Beth exclaimed. "Seems like foolish myths to me."

"Myths?" Elijah said back, confused at how Beth was responding to their nation's beliefs. "You hear giant serpents sing in a language only you can understand. Who are you to talk of myths?"

"I believe it," Beth began, "because I know it is real. I have seen it, heard it, and experienced it for myself."

"You will see that what I am saying is truth," Elijah challenged her. "No enemy, no matter their strength, will be able to stop us, because we have divine protection. If what I believe is true, then we will be protected on this journey, and we will safely make it back to your home."

"We have enough skill to do that on our own," Beth spoke back to Elijah. "So we will see what is demonstrated, if there is anything needed to be displayed."

"Enough of that," Royce jumped in, ending their quarrel. "Tell her how you were offered this journey. Surely, you must have been sons of great men to have been in the council of those who would send you forth to find the armor you are searching for."

"My father was a strong warrior," Jeremiah shared, trying to win Beth's attention. "He was one of the greatest generals in our king's army. He died defending our country in the greatest battle of his time."

"And you?" Beth asked Jeremiah, wanting to know more about him, her attention being won. "What do you do back home?"

"I too serve in a high position over our kingdom's army," Jeremiah said, his eyes looking into Beth's from across where they sat. "I am the captain over our entire military."

"So are you a prince, then?" Royce stepped in.

"No," Jeremiah answered.

"Any form of royalty?" Royce asked, attempting to make Jeremiah seem distasteful in Beth's sight.

"No," Jeremiah spoke back, in a softer tone this time.

"Then, you are just a servant in your homeland?" Royce questioned, throwing his final blow at Jeremiah's pride.

"Yes," Jeremiah barely breathed, an anger stirring up on the inside of him because of being embarrassed in front of Beth.

"Royce!" Elijah hissed at his friend. "You know Jeremiah is a great warrior. He's one of the greatest our homeland has ever seen, and he was sent to protect me."

"What's so special about you?" Beth asked Elijah. "Why must

you be protected?"

"I…" Elijah hesitated to explain. "I am just much weaker than Jeremiah. I would not have made it this far without him."

"Well then," Beth began to ask another question, unsatisfied with Elijah's previous answer, "who is your father?"

"He…" Elijah spoke, becoming trapped by the questions. "He is a strong leader amongst our people. He helped organize this journey Jeremiah and I are now on."

Elijah paused to see if Royce would ask him the same questions he had asked Jeremiah, but Royce would not, because he already saw Elijah as a dear friend, and his questions for Jeremiah were only birthed out of jealousy.

"We should rest," Elijah said, trying to end the conversation. "There is still a long journey ahead of us. It would be foolish to waste our energy on talking."

With that, the four of them went to lay in separate areas of the caves, sleeping on the dirt filled ground that was warm to the touch. The crackling flames around the cavern lulled them to sleep, as the moon hid away behind heavy clouds and smoke in the skies outside, leaving the desert valleys in darkness, the glowing of the fire pits illuminated in the distance.

In the morning, they went on with their journey, leaving the fires they lit in the caves to remain burning. As the day went on, the temperature continued to rise, leaving their foreheads to shine with sweat, and their hair greased. The scent of the burning oil could faintly be noticed as they walked through the great clearing. The earth beneath the hooves of their horses had turned to black ash, and there was no sign of any form of life anywhere near them.

"When the four founders established Terrabeth," Royce began to tell the two foreigners as the four travelers rode their horses side by side, "at the end of the Age of Chaos, as our historians call it, the rebel forces that were defeated fled to this region."

"What was it they were rebelling against?" Elijah asked.

"Order, and set government," Royce spoke, talking loudly over the scarf that still covered his mouth. "They hated the idea of laws, and submitting to these laws even more. After the final battle to bring forth the Age of Kingship, which is the age we still now live in, the surviving rebels came to hide in the caverns of the valleys surrounding the Northern Fire Pits."

"Where are they now?" Elijah questioned.

"That was many generations ago," Royce responded. "They've long since died away."

"It was not age that killed them," Beth spoke up as they reached midday, the black paint around her eyes smeared across her face due to her sweat.

"Were they hunted down?" Jeremiah asked, riding to the left

side of Beth.

"Not by men," Beth responded, causing Elijah and Jeremiah to become confused.

"Then by who?" Elijah asked, his curiosity running rampant.

"It's said there used to be wild beasts that roamed these valleys," Royce confessed. "Large lizard-like creatures that could stand on two legs like men, but gallop on all four legs like horses. Technically, they have not been seen for a time now. Many believe they died off long ago, as well."

"This valley is a wasteland, that can't even grow weeds," Jeremiah said loudly. "Could they have all starved off?"

"They were preyed on," Beth said, making sure Royce could not hide the potential danger the four of them were now in, "by beasts greater than them."

"…And what beasts are those?" Elijah asked, now worried for his safety in what had first seemed like an easy passage to the belt.

"You will see soon," Royce spoke. "So long as we have the princess with us, we should be guarded."

"How is it you can protect us?" Elijah asked, looking to Beth, his eyes squinting as sweat dripped into their corners.

"Don't worry," Beth told Elijah as they carried on toward the fire pits. "If times become desperate, you will find out for yourself."

That evening, they reached the base of the range of the fire pits. The Northern Fire Pits were several mountains, all at different heights, with their peaks cut away, exposing the pools of oil they were filled with, and atop the surface of the oil burned an everlasting fire. The pit they needed to get to was at the center of the range of fire pits, surrounded by all the other ones. Though this one was a little lower than the others around it, its pit was much wider, and its pool much deeper.

Even though nighttime was not visible to them, because they were in the continuous shadow of the black smoky sky, lit by the endless light of the fire pits, their bodies could sense it was time to rest. Despite the fact that there was plenty of light to see them through to the pit that held the belt, they had grown tired from the travelling, and drained from the burning heat of the area they were in. They decided to seek refuge in a cavern like they had the night before, bringing light to it the same way they had in the previous cavern.

"What's wrong?" Elijah asked Jeremiah as he approached Jeremiah, who was standing at the narrow entrance to the cavern that they had already been settled in for hours now.

"Something's not right," Jeremiah told him, as the two looked around the well-lit land surrounding the cavern entrance.

"What gives you reason to think this?" Elijah asked Jeremiah, who he now had begun to see as a friend, and not just a guardian on this journey.

"Just a feeling," Jeremiah honestly answered, hoping that Elijah would trust his instincts. "I feel like we are being followed."

While they spoke, Beth and Royce stood deep in the cave with the horses that were becoming restless, neighing and puffing steam from their flaring nostrils.

"What has gotten into you four?" Beth gently spoke, moving her arms about, petting their faces, trying to calm them down. "Be calmed. There is nothing a matter."

With that, the horses began to quiet themselves, finding peace in Beth's soothing voice and touch.

"It must be the heat of the fire pits," Royce said, petting his horse's neck. "They aren't used to this environment."

"None of us are," Beth spoke softly, as she began to tie the horses to small boulders that were piled along the cavern wall, with the ropes that were used by their riders to steer them when they were ridden, tying Royce's horse first. "This place is terrible; truly a grave for those rebels."

"You've calmed them down," Royce reassured Beth as she knotted Elijah's horse's rope. "Why do you still tie them down?"

"In case they are startled again," Beth answered as she bound Jeremiah's horse to a boulder. "I'm sure they will get stirred up all over again if danger comes our way."

"I won't let any danger come to you," Royce said, causing Beth to stop what she was doing, leaving the last horse to be untied, her whole body turning to Royce.

"We've already talked about this, Royce," Beth said, Royce taking a step toward her.

"You would stay bitter, and not forgive me?" Royce combated her feelings with his words. "You would hold on to your grief, and never give the opportunity to regain what we once shared?"

"Royce," Beth said, nearly unable to respond. "Why now, Royce? Why now that it has been years for my clay emotions to harden into stone? You chose to leave, and this is the consequence of that choice."

"No, Beth," Royce said, grabbing hold of her hands, "I won't leave you again."

"You are already scheduled to leave once we get back to the palace," Beth argued, not pulling her hands from him. "And so, again, you will leave me."

"Then come with me," Royce excitedly spoke. "Come with me to Terrashin, and wherever else I am to go."

"I can't, Royce," Beth said to him, the precious stone over her forehead shimmering in the waving flames around them. "I can't leave my father alone with Darius. I feel that I am the only one holding back his wickedness from fully devouring our nation."

"You can't," Royce challenged her, "or you won't?"

With that, Beth pulled her hands from his, and walked away from Royce and the four horses that were still standing calmly, while Elijah and Jeremiah walked back into the cave where the others were.

"Jeremiah has an uneasy feeling," Elijah informed Royce as they walked up to him, Beth now lying down in a corner of the cave, prepared to fall asleep. "He thinks we're being followed."

"Could the western armies have been tracking us?" Royce asked him, remembering the stories the two foreigners had shared with him.

"No," Jeremiah answered, "that's not it."

"Then what is it?" Royce asked Jeremiah, relying on his warrior skills that had yet to come into their full maturity.

"I don't know," Jeremiah admitted. "I just feel as though we are being tracked. What were those beasts you spoke of?"

"No," Royce told him, "they've long since been extinct."

"What about the other beasts that caused their extinction?" Elijah asked. "Could it be them?"

"No," Royce said. "Those beasts do not come to these areas

of the fire pits. They are bound to other places."

"Then what could it be?" Jeremiah returned a question to Royce.

"My brother is an evil man, with matchlessly evil schemes," Royce confessed to them, talking softly so that Beth could not hear his words. "He may have sent spies. Whether to watch us or kill us, I don't know."

"Why would he do such a terrible thing to us?" Elijah questioned. "Including you, his brother, and Beth, the princess of all people, in such a horrible plot."

"Before I first left Terrabeth, he was planning much worse things," Royce spoke, releasing secrets he thought would die alongside with him. "His heart is not for our nation, or our king. It's for his own benefit."

"He must be stopped," Elijah boldly said.

"He can't be," Royce explained hopelessly. "He has gained too much control and influence. We need to quickly do what we must in Terrabeth, and in Terrashin, so to speedily be on our way before he begins any of his plans. Once we have finished our commitments to him, we must flee from where he can reach us. If not, your journey to find the six pieces of armor could be delayed."

"We will do what we must," Jeremiah sternly spoke, looking back toward the short tunnel that led to the entrance of the cave.

"For tonight, the three of us will each take a turn guarding the entry way to this cave. If anyone tries to enter, they will be seen, and the watchman will wake the others up to fight the intruder."

Royce sat watch for the first third of the night, followed by Jeremiah who watched during the second third. Nobody came by the entrance, and nothing caused either of them to become alarmed.

During the last third of the night, Elijah took his position by the entrance to the cave, sitting a few feet into the tunnel. His tired eyes looked out to the wide pathways around the fire pits, overlaid with dirt that had been burnt black, with jagged boulders scattered around. The moon was blocked out by the massive clouds of black smoke high above the pits, but the pits themselves were lit up by the burning flames beneath the smoke.

Through the night, the heat from the fire pits above and around them had kept him from falling asleep for longer than a whole hour at a time, leaving Elijah now barely able to stay awake. Unable to hold the weight of his eyelids, they slowly began to roll up and down over his eyes, his will trying to keep them open, until he gave way to his tiredness, and his eyelids shut.

The soft sounds of small rocks and pebbles falling suddenly caused his eyes to swing open, his whole body jolting forward, forcefully waking himself up. His eyes opened in time to see a small cloud of ash and dust rising from the ground on the right side of the entrance, as if it had been kicked up.

Jumping to his feet, Elijah drew his sword, slowly pacing forward to the cave's entrance, his sword held out ahead of him, pointing in the direction he was walking toward.

Without warning, a few loose rocks rolled over the cave entrance, falling from the outside of the tunnel, a small trail of dust and ash following behind them, all landing on the ground at the foot of the entrance.

"Who goes there?!" Elijah shouted loudly, his voice echoing through the cave, growing in volume as it did, waking the three others that were sleeping, and startling the four horses.

Quickly, Jeremiah and Royce got to their feet, racing to Elijah's side, as Beth rose to calm the horses that began to panic even more than they had earlier.

Elijah ran out of the tunnel, spinning around to look above the entrance, to find nothing.

"Be calm," Beth told the horses as they pulled at the ropes that were holding them down. "Be calm."

Her own horse, which had not been tied down like the other three, began to thrash about more wildly than the others, suddenly shooting off, heading toward the exit of the cave, flying past Royce and Jeremiah.

"Elijah!" Jeremiah cried out to the prince who was directly in the path of the oncoming horse that was bulleting towards him.

Elijah quickly jumped out of the way, the horse plowing through the spot where he was just standing a breath ago. From the ground where he landed, he watched as the horse shot off northward, leaving a trailing cloud of rising dust behind it.

Jeremiah and Royce ran out of the cave, their swords pointed out, the both of them scanning the area, their eyes darting around nearly as quickly as the runaway horse.

"What happened?" Jeremiah quickly asked Elijah as he got back onto his feet.

"Someone was out here," Elijah said, looking around for signs of the person who had woke him up. "They were climbing over the outside entrance of the cave, knocking down rocks as they did."

"Did you see them?" Royce quickly asked, wanting a description.

"No," Elijah answered, his heart still beating rapidly. "I didn't."

"We must quickly leave this place," Jeremiah ordered, running into the cave, the other two running after him.

"What is happening?" Beth quickly questioned them as the three men untied their horses and climbed up onto them.

"We don't know," Jeremiah said, directing his horse toward the cave exit, "but it's not good."

"Here," Royce said to Beth, extending his hand to her as he sat on his horse. "Take my hand, and climb onto my horse. Yours has fled."

Hesitating inwardly, Beth did as she was told, climbing onto the horse with Royce. Her arms tightly wrapped across his stomach as they prepared to rush out of the cave.

Immediately, Royce and Beth rode the horse out of the cave, with Elijah and Jeremiah following behind them. Once they left the cave, they rode through the wide path going northward, toward the pit that they needed to get to. Soon enough, they found themselves running through the cloud of dust left by Beth's horse, but, after a few moments, the kicked up dust led to a different direction than where they were going, trailing off to a path on their right side.

"He went the other way!" Beth yelled into Royce's ear as they continued racing forward.

"We're not going after him!" Royce yelled back as the bottom of the particular fire pit they had come to visit became visible in the distance. "It's too dangerous. If anything, that horse will help us by leading our attackers away from us."

Suddenly, Beth's horse could be heard as it released a terrifying cry in the far distance, as though it were being slaughtered, with its painful screeches echoing throughout the fire pits.

"What did they do to it?!" Elijah cried out as they drew closer to the base of the fire pit they were about to climb up.

Royce had no answer for Elijah. Without slowing down, they reached the base of the fire pit, and began to ride their horses up the steep slope, their specially designed hooves enabling them to quickly race upward at an angle, while the riders leaned forward on their horses. Soon after, they reached a small plateau area where they could briefly catch their breath, allowing their horses a chance to regain their strength.

"Royce!" Beth loudly said as the four stood beside their horses. "What was that?"

"He believes them to be Darius' men," Jeremiah answered for Royce as Elijah noticed a large lump of something left on the ground, away from where they stood.

"Has he plotted to kill us?" Beth asked enraged as Elijah unnoticeably walked in silence toward what he saw.

"Nothing is certain," Royce said, trying to calm Beth down as Elijah reached his discovery. "Darius' men potentially stalking us is the only explanation I can think of."

Elijah knelt down, looking closely at what he found, the stench of rotting flesh oozing out from it. He could see exposed bones sticking out of the pile that was only a few feet long.

"Look!" Elijah called to them, noticing bite marks in the flesh of the carcass that was decomposing before him.

"What is it?" Jeremiah asked, rushing over with the other two, standing over Elijah.

"My horse!" Beth gasped, disturbed and nauseated by the finding.

"No," Royce said, pushing Elijah aside, and kneeling at the finding, "this body has been here for some time now. Its skin has no hair, and looks smooth."

Royce reached his hand down to the dirt around the body, stroking his fingers through the dirt, feeling for more evidence. His hands quickly came across heavy stones. Scooping them up into his hands, the ash and dirt covering them began to fall away between his open fingers, exposing the stones to be rubies.

Royce quickly dropped them, and fell backward fearfully.

"We must go," Royce told them, rushing back to the horses. "Now!"

As they all jumped back onto their horses, a rattling sound began to ring out from beneath them, shaking up fear within the bones of the travelers.

"What is that sound?" Jeremiah asked as he looked down the mountain, seeing what appeared to be sets of glowing red eyes shining from the path they had come up through, far behind them.

"Hurry!" Royce roared as their horses all shot off, climbing up the mountain side, zigzagging their way toward the top that was still a distance away.

As they passed the halfway point of the lower standing mountain, the rattling continued, almost intensifying. At no point did any of the riders look back, for fear of losing balance at this steep height. The heat from the top of the pit they were climbing up began to intensify so greatly that their clothes became soaked in their sweat, with ash from the smoke above latching onto their faces.

"We're almost there!" Royce managed to yell out as they neared the rim of the pit, feeling the drain on his energy from the furnace-like heat, while the rattling began to become louder.

Elijah's horse, trailing at the end of the group, made a turn to climb up at another angle, following the other two horses, and as it did, Elijah looked back to see two massive lizard-like figures racing after them, not far behind him and his horse. Their bodies were hard to distinguish, because they were nearly the same color as the earth they raced across, but he could see their two sets of eyes, like glowing rubies dowsed in flames.

Soon, they reached the top rim of the fire pit, its massive flames burning across the surface of the pool of oil, enraged with a fire that could not be quenched, and was barely contained by the pit itself.

"Keep moving!" Elijah screamed from behind the other two horses as they began to ride across the rim of the pool of fire. "They are gaining on us!"

The rattling became so loud that even Royce, at the head of the group, could easily distinguish it over the sounds of the roaring flames that were calling from the fire pit they had climbed.

Without warning, Elijah's horse slightly leapt up, dodging a large stone in its way, causing Elijah to lose grip of the horse, and slide off its backside. Elijah's thrown body rolled across the ground, covering his entire body with ashy dirt as he spun across the narrow rim, while his group unknowingly raced away without him.

His body became still, leaving him on his left side, looking in the direction he had been coming from. Slowly approaching him were the two beasts that he had watched chasing after them. They were nearly his size, walking on all four legs, their long black claws digging into the dirt, as long thin tails dragged behind them. Their bodies were covered in dark scales of charcoal, with long spiked feathers of black poking out from their spines. Their faces were long, with their top row of razor teeth poking out from their closed mouths.

Barely breathing, Elijah slowly stood to his feet as the two beasts froze themselves about fifteen steps away from the prince. His hand slowly moved onto the handle of his sword, which was safely placed in its sheath, while the four eyes of the lizards focused on Elijah's moving hand.

As he gripped his sword, the two lizards rose up, standing on their hind legs, making themselves as tall as Elijah. The rattling that had fallen silent began to sound again from within their throats, this time in a much lower pitch, causing their long thick necks to vibrate and stretch out.

Suddenly, one of the fierce lizards lunged at Elijah, but as it did, an eruption from the fire pit they stood beside sounded, and the massive head of what looked to be a songvis shot out, its mouth wide open, capturing the lizard in its jaws. This songvis was not like the others Elijah had seen. It was much larger in size, with smooth black skin, and red rubies across its neck. In place of black rings around its eyes were white rings, and its teeth like sharpened swords.

As the captured lizard was swallowed, the second lizard threw itself onto the giant head of the beast that came from the fire, and sunk its small teeth into its face. The brilliant rubies across the neck of the larger beast began to shine like falling stars as it roared out in pain, slamming its head into the ground, squashing the lizard with great force, and then retreating back into the Fire Pit.

"Elijah!" Jeremiah yelled as they raced up to Elijah from behind.

"Move away from the pit!" Beth screamed at Elijah as they neared him.

Before he could react, the same beast shot back up out of the flames, its neck fully extended out of the pool of oil. Looking down to Elijah, its face slowly crept toward him, coming to a stop several feet away.

Elijah removed his hand from holding the sword's handle, and his eyes looked into the eyes of the beast, settling the fear within him, not backing away from this terrifyingly sized monster.

The jaws of the beast suddenly opened wide, and a powerful roar came pummeling out, releasing itself over Elijah, but he courageously remained standing, unmoved by the powerful beast that could easily devour him at any moment. His hands tightly bound themselves into heavy fists, and the beating of his heart echoed throughout the fire pits as the brightness of the rubies on the beast's neck radiated a brilliant light onto Elijah.

The beast then lifted its head higher, still looking down to Elijah, as the other travelers watched from over a dozen steps away, in awe of the great beast that then fell silent, with its stones dim.

The rubies across its neck slowly lit again, trickling upward, to its face, and then the beast began to sing a song, its notes low and flat sounding. The giant ruby atop its forehead began to glow as the melody poured over the area.

Elijah closed his eyes, hearing the bellowing notes of the animal as Beth walked up beside Elijah, the precious stone over her head glowing a brilliant shade of red.

"Chosen one, from the land past the sea," Beth began to sing beside Elijah who stood frozen, listening to Beth sing aloud the interpretation. "Who has embarked on this quest, hear the song that I sing. Your journey will test, your worthiness of the throne, for from the forest, comes a king once foretold. Within the pages, that you hold in your grasp, holds the answers to questions; their origin the past."

"Please," Elijah spoke, opening his eyes, looking up to the magnificent beast above him. "I've come for the belt. May I have it?"

The beast responded to him in song, astonished by Elijah's bravery.

"The first of the six, I will give to you now," Beth interpreted with her shaking hands at her sides. "And with it great power, worn by owners of crowns; from your kingdom alone men of royal decent, any other wearers will soon meet their end."

The long neck of the beast then slid back beneath the flames, leaving the four speechless on the rim of the fire pit, with moments passing as they waited, frozen where they stood, none daring to say a single word.

The beast's head slid out from the raging flames once more, with a stunning silver belt hanging from its closed lips, shimmering in the spiraling flames. The beast lowered its face to Elijah, dangling the precious belt before him. Elijah stretched out his shaking hands toward the belt, taking hold of it, feeling tremendous power surge into him, as though all the life of his youth had filled him at one moment. The beast released the belt, and Elijah completely took it into his possession, pulling it toward him, his eyes fixated on its elegant design. Though it was the sturdiest of material, it was nearly weightless in his hands. The beast backed away, continuing to look down to Elijah, as dozens of other heads like the one looking down on his began to rise up from the fiery pool, all their eyes fixed on the young prince who bravely stood before them, with the belt they had guarded for ages in his hands.

The first beast then sang, again.

"We were chosen to guard this gift you've received," Beth turned the notes into words. "You were chosen to take it, to vanquish enemies. Though the night it may fall, and the dark has its reign, the sun will soon rise, and put evil to shame."

All the beasts then looked up to the clouds of smoke above them that were as black as night, and began to cry out horribly loud roars, the rubies across their necks burning sensationally, nearly blinding the four travelers, forcing them to shut their eyes as their horses began to cry out, kicking about, not out of fear, but in joining the forceful melody.

Accompanied with this swarm of beasts were hundreds of others just like them, across the many other fire pits, roaring at the black smoke, their rubies lighting the peaks of every fire pit, like exploding stars.

Elijah lifted his head toward the sky, barely opening his eyes to see the thick cloud of smoke beginning to part above the pit. The beasts all ended their song at once, their roars echoing for several seconds, ringing throughout the atmosphere, as the light emitting from their glowing rubies died away, none left glowing in the dancing flames. Elijah then opened his eyes wide to see a great divide in the smoke clouds, beginning right above them, and stretching back over the path they had taken through the range of Northern Fire Pits, and across the desert valley. The rays of the hidden sun were shining down, lighting the whole trail from the sky to the earth.

The first beast then sang one final song.

"This path will light your way, so you may go in peace," Beth repeated in a way the other three could understand. "It will keep danger away, you may leave here with ease. We now look to the one, who holds hope in his hands. On your way you must go, to more foreign lands."

"Thank you," Elijah quietly told the beast, smiling, rejuvenated with hope for the future, as Beth's stone became dim.

Elijah placed the belt in his supply bag as the others all then returned to their seats on their horses, none saying a word, and began to slowly trot away. The beasts from every fire pit watched them as they continued on their pilgrimage that would take them across the world, in hopes to save the Kingdom of Abel.

As the group began to travel down the fire pit, the beasts harmoniously all began to sing a familiar tune, in honor of the departure of Elijah and his companions. Elijah smiled, and began to sing words along to their musical notes.

"Let faith guide your steps, and hope guard your heart," Elijah began to sing joyfully, the song of his homeland even bringing a smile to Jeremiah, as they rode away. "May peace bring you rest, as light binds the dark. From the sky comes our King, our hope in the east. He'll shelter us all, our worries He'll ease. There's hope in the east."

Newly Crowned King

A thin sheet of stars that seemed like scattered specks of dust began to become visible along the edge of the sky that touched the top rim of the east side of the fog barrier as Micah sat in a tree that grew along the eastern rim of the wide meadow. From where he sat, he could see five other spies, hidden in the tall thick weeds of the meadow, their stomachs to the ground, the whole group keeping watch for intruders to seep out from the dense fog.

Bored from sitting alone at his post since dawn that morning, Micah had begun to carve a piece of freshly cut wood into what would eventually be a flute that would be no longer than his hand. He had been set at this post shortly after Jeremiah had left the Kingdom of Abel, sitting in the tree as long as the sun was out, rotating with another warrior at nightfall. This job was simple to do, since there was no sign of the western army coming through the barrier, and not a sound had been heard from the thick mist. It had been nearly a month since this meadow was been filled with the warriors of east and west, fighting until daybreak.

Micah puckered his lips together, blowing loose wooden dust off of his carving, clearing away the dust to expose the beginnings of a detailed olive branch engraved on the bottom side of the flute.

"Micah," a voice whispered from beneath him, causing him to look down to see the warrior who sat in this tree during the nighttime hours squatting on the ground, staying behind the tree's wide trunk, keeping himself out of view from the west side.

"You're here just in time," Micah whispered back, filling his pocket with his knife and flute, while the sunlight began to diminish. "I've become restless, even more so than usual."

"Still nothing, then?" the warrior asked as Micah began to slowly lower himself, making sure his body could not be seen from the west side as he climbed down the tree.

"Of course not," Micah breathed out frustrated. "Not a single sign of anything."

"I suppose that's best," the warrior said as he looked up to Micah while five other warriors in other trees along the meadow began to trade out as well. "I would rather be frustrated from boredom than come into contact with those soulless rebels on any occasion."

"Not if it meant we could end this war," Micah responded,

reaching the bottom of the tree, standing next to the warrior who was to take his position.

"Do you really think we can win this war?" the warrior asked Micah, knowing how strong the western army had become, especially with Plague on their side.

"Of course I do," Micah comforted his fellow soldier, placing his hand on his shoulder. "There's always hope in the east."

"Does your brother have anything planned, yet?" the warrior asked Micah about Jeremiah. "I don't think I've seen him the entire time we have been posted out here. I heard he is in the palace with the king, planning a means of attacking the western armies, but, I would think if we had a chance, we would have already begun acting upon it."

"Some plans just take time to come together," Micah spoke, his brother being mentioned causing him to miss Jeremiah, "but once they come together, their success outshines the process it took to be obtained. We will be fine. Don't worry."

Without a word, the warrior nodded his head to Micah, and began his steady climb up the tree, taking his post for the night. Micah then turned his body toward the east, and at the moment he took his first step, the warrior spoke to him.

"Get down!" the warrior loudly whispered.

Reacting to this, Micah quickly fell to the ground, positioning himself against the back of the tree trunk. He slightly peaked out his face to take a look at the meadow, and saw a black crow darting through the sky. Its long feathery wings cut through the air as the crow zigzagged across the meadow, with blazing red eyes taking note of all the warriors who were attempting to hide, both in the clearing, and in the trees.

Shortly after, the crow flew into the fog barrier, where it had first come from.

Moments passed, and then the sound of a deep drum began to erupt from within the fog barrier, slamming at a rhythm that was drastically slower than the beating hearts of the eastern warriors whose thoughts were beginning to fill with uncertainty. Micah kept watching the fog barrier as he began to see what looked like two floating orange flares becoming brighter as they neared the end of the fog barrier.

Seconds later, the two glowing orbs from within the fog barrier made their way out, and into plain sight, exposing themselves to be two fires burning on the end of long torches, held by extremely tall men, dressed in the normal western warrior armor. Around their waists were long leather chords that stretched behind them, reaching into the fog. Moments later, a large iron carriage came out from the fog, being pulled by the leather chords attached to these men. The carriage had no top, was the shape of a half sphere, the round side facing down, with three wheels rolling it, and inside the carriage sat Oliver.

Micah's jaw dropped as he saw Oliver, who was wearing a bronze crown over his head, designed just like Olivia's. He was dressed in his normal commanding armor, but now also had a royal silver woven cape hanging over his left shoulder, pinned up with a round onyx badge. Proudly sitting, with his head slightly tilted upward, he looked forward. On his right shoulder sat the crow that had just been in the meadow. It was no secret to the eastern warriors that this was one of the two western Diadem.

After reaching about halfway into the meadow, the two giant men and the carriage came to a stop. Oliver stood up, standing high in the center of the carriage.

"We know how many of you there are," Oliver pronounced loudly, his voice echoing through the meadow, being heard by all the eastern warriors, "and we know where you are."

The warriors, stunned by fear, silently waited to see what was to come next.

"I tell you this," Oliver continued to speak powerfully, "if but one will take the message I have to your king, I will spare your lives."

There was no response from any of the eastern warriors.

"The words I have to deliver to your king could save your own lives, as well as the lives of your loved ones." Oliver enticed the men to come out from their hiding.

One of the warriors leapt up from his position in the middle of the meadow, popping out from beneath the tall grass, with a readied bow and arrow in his hands. Without a moment to lose, he shot his arrow toward Oliver.

Just as quickly as the bow shot through the air, the Diadem flew off Oliver's shoulder, grabbed the arrow that was coming at his master, broke it with the grip of its talons, and darted after the eastern warrior. Within the blink on an eye, the crow had clawed at the eastern warrior, causing his heavily wounded body to collapse to the ground. As this happened, another warrior followed the first one, shooting an arrow at Oliver, but then finding the same fate with the Diadem as the first warrior had. This happened three more times, finishing off all the warriors that had been positioned throughout the meadow within several seconds.

"I gave you the opportunity to save your own lives," Oliver growled out, "and now five lay dead where countless warriors before have been buried! I will ask again: Will any of you fools deliver my message to the king, or must you all die, leaving me to deliver the message to him myself?!"

Micah's knees weakly pushed his body up, forcing himself to stand. With courage fighting to be known in his heart, he took his first step out from behind the tree, and began to walk out into the meadow, causing Oliver to turn his eyes to him as the Diadem returned to Oliver's right shoulder.

"Finally," Oliver yelled out for the other eastern warriors to hear, "a man who does not lack sense."

Micah kept his eyes fixed on Oliver, who was staring back with the same level of intensity, as Micah approached the sharp edged carriage that was about six feet high. The warriors pulling the carriage looked forward, as their rusty helmets covered their faces, ignoring Micah.

"What is your name, warrior?" Oliver asked, looking down to Micah as he reached the carriage.

"Micah," he bravely answered back to Oliver, defiance stirring in his eyes.

"Well then, Micah," Oliver continued to speak, his deep voice carrying through the air as night fell over the meadow, "take this message to your king, and let him know it is from King Oliver, of the Kingdom of Cain. I demand he give himself over, as a prisoner, here, at this very spot in one month, or I will retrieve him from his own palace myself."

Without breaking his stare with Micah, Oliver rose both his hands up into the air, and immediately countless amounts of roaring warriors cried out from within the fog barrier, as though many rushing waterfalls had been let loose, each warrior hidden within the fog yelling out as loud as he could. The ground beneath Micah's feet trembled, while the wrathful shouts of the western army could be heard miles away, deep into the eastern territory.

Oliver then lowered his arms, causing the reckless cheering to fall silent, leaving a wake of fear over all those who had heard it.

"And I will not be alone," Oliver smirked, looking down to Micah whose face had become terrified by the warning battle cry.

Without another word, Oliver sat back down, and the warriors bound to his carriage then turned around, walking back into the fog barrier, pulling their king behind them. Micah watched them disappear back into the fog, hopelessness knocking on the door of his heart; the courage within him pondered opening the door.

"And where was Olivia?" Seth questioned Micah, who was standing before him while Seth sat on his seat in the throne room of the Kingdom of Abel, two nights after Micah's encounter with Oliver.

"I do not know, my king," Micah informed Seth, with the doors to the room shut, having only these two and Benjamin, who was standing next to Seth's throne, in the entire room. "He only made himself known."

"Perhaps she was overthrown," Benjamin spoke, turning to the king. "Whether by Oliver or the great monster she released, she may no longer be in power. Truthfully, I cannot imagine such a threat on behalf of the west being done by anyone else but her, unless she were to be dead."

"There is still much to consider," Seth responded to Benjamin, overwhelmed by the news Micah had brought him.

"Where is Jeremiah?" Micah asked the king, eager to see his brother whom he missed. "It has been so long since I have seen him. I would like to speak with him."

"He is not available now," Seth sternly responded, still keeping Elijah and Jeremiah's journey secretive.

"When may I see him?" Micah asked, hoping to soon reunite with his brother.

"Do you have anything else to report to us?" Benjamin asked Micah, ignoring his questions about his brother.

"No," Micah responded unsatisfied.

"You have done us well," Seth spoke to the young musician. "Your father would be very proud were he here to see you. But now, you must return to your position alongside the meadow. You may stay in the city for tonight, but you are to return for the meadow at dawn."

"Thank you, my king," Micah said, bowing before Seth, and then quickly walking out of the throne room.

Seth and Benjamin remained silent until Micah left the room, and the door shut behind him.

"I will not let them take you, my friend," Benjamin tried to comfort Seth, placing his large wrinkly hand on Seth's shoulder, "we will find a way."

"If there is no way," Seth began to speak boldly, prepared for what could come, "then I will gladly hand myself over to the west in order to protect the east. My people will not fall victim to the western army because I cowered away."

"I have advised you for decades now," Benjamin continued to try to uplift his king. "Though these are the darkest times we have seen in your reign, we will not cower away, nor fall to any sword forged in the west. You have had my allegiance, and will have it still, until I breathe my last breath."

"Thank you, my friend," Seth breathed out, placing his hand on Benjamin's hand that was still resting on Seth's shoulder, gripping it tightly. "We will find a way."

A banging came from the massive entrance door to the throne room, echoing through the marble room.

"Enter." Seth called out, the door immediately yet slowly pushing open into the room.

"King Seth!" one of Mary's five maidens called out to Seth, forcing her way into the throne room, rushing up to the foot of the platform where he sat. "You must come quickly! The queen, she has collapsed!"

Without a moment to spare, Seth and Benjamin began to rush to

271

where the other four maidens had taken Mary, placing her in a bedroom near where she had collapsed.

"What exactly happened?" Seth asked her as they hurried through the long halls.

"We do not know," the young maiden answered, leading the way. "We were all walking behind her, and she just fell unconscious. We were able to carry her into a nearby room to lay her down."

The maiden then walked up to an open door, leading Seth and Benjamin into the room where Mary was in bed, sitting up, surrounded by her four other maidens.

"Mary," Seth said, sitting at her bed side, grabbing a hold of her tired hands, "what has happened?"

"I am fine," Mary argued, seeming to act healthy. "I just became a bit dizzy, and lost my balance. Really, this is unnecessary."

"Are you tired?" Seth asked, seeing that her eyes were hiding sickness within her aged body. "What caused you to become dizzy?"

"Seth, I just lost my balance for a moment," Mary disputed, trying to convince her husband, and all around her, that she was in good health. "I am fine now."

"Let us get you to our bed then," Seth said, standing from the bed, he and the maidens helping Mary out of the bed, and onto her feet.

As soon as she stood up, she wrapped her right arm around Seth's, and he could feel her pulling on him, trying to keep her balance, while the maidens around her stretched their arms out, ready to catch or hold her up if she began to sway.

"Let us be on our way then," Mary spoke, catching her breath as she and Seth slowly began to walk out of the room.

It took nearly an hour for Mary to be taken up to her room where her maidens set her in bed for the night, leaving her alone in the room with Seth, who sat again at her side on the edge of the bed.

"When will he be here?" Mary eerily asked Seth, the few candles lit in their room burning still.

"When will he be here?" Seth repeated her question back to her confused, not quite sure how Mary could have known Oliver had threatened to come to the palace.

"Yes," Mary spoke weakly, her eyes now closed as she went on. "When will our son return?"

"I don't know, Mary," Seth sighed with relief, glad that the threatening news had not yet reached his ailing wife. "The journey we sent him on will take him quite a while to finish. Really, it's only begun."

"I miss him," Mary honestly confessed, saddened that she had not seen her son in about a month.

"As do I, Mary," Seth told her as her shoulders sunk down, her body falling asleep. "As do I."

After waiting for a few minutes to better solidify Mary entering into slumber, Seth stood up from their bed, and walked toward the exit doors, planning to go to the sacred garden to receive peace and direction amidst the spiraling storm that was resting over his thoughts. His entire life he had relied on his hope to see him through, and could always see a way in which the rising odds against him would fail to overtake him, but in these darkest of hours, his sight was dimming. He could not see a way in which his kingdom could prevail against the western army.

Departing Terrabeth

"What is it you're looking for?" Beth asked Jeremiah as the two sat in the royal garden within the palace of Terrabeth, the bright full moon radiating down into the garden, with its beams reflecting off of the wide lake that took up most of the garden area, while the royal songvis took rest beneath the depths of the water.

The group had all returned to the capital city after several days of safe travel, returning from their time at the Northern Fire Pits. They had returned to Phillip's palace earlier that day, and were planning to rest there for at least one night. The three men were prepared to depart for the next continent on their long journey, while Beth was to remain within the stone walls of the palace that had contained her her whole life.

After their silent dinner, Elijah left to his room for the night, and Royce had momentarily vanished off with his two brothers, leaving Jeremiah alone with Beth in the royal garden that was placed on the opposite side of the back wall of King Phillip's throne room.

"Well," Jeremiah gently responded to the princess, "you know what it is I am looking for. I need the armor to save my homeland."

"No," Beth corrected Jeremiah's understanding, as the several short palm trees around them stood still, unmoved due to the absence of wind in this open area that had no roof. "You are looking for something much more than these pieces of armor. I can see it in your eyes. You could find all these pieces of armor twice, and yet still be looking for what I'm asking you about. It is what's driving you to complete this journey."

"What drives me is knowing that I would have made my father proud in successfully guarding Elijah," Jeremiah shyly admitted to the princess he had become very fond of. "I am his legacy, and I hope to leave as great an example for my future sons after me, just as my father did."

Gentle calls began to rise from the large body of water, and calm rays of light began to reflect from the water depths, with ripples spiraling out across the lake's surface, drawing Beth's attention as the two sat on the edge of the lake, her sharp chin now pointed toward the water.

"You will," Beth said turning back to Jeremiah, smiling, as the songvis' calls and lights disappeared into the night.

"What did she say?" Jeremiah asked Beth, returning a smile, causing his stubbly face to form into a position it rarely held.

"You will see soon enough," Beth said, looking away from Jeremiah, hiding away her thin lips that were arching upward, and then gracefully stood to her feet. "You will see."

"Why won't you tell me?" he asked her in a friendly manor, looking up to her smooth face that was outlined by the moonbeams reflecting off the lake.

"Sometimes the future is better played out as an unraveling mystery, rather than executing a well-crafted plot," she answered, leaving Jeremiah on the ground. "And besides, it's getting late. You have a long journey ahead of you in the morning."

"Come with us," Jeremiah spat out, quickly standing to his feet, leaving Beth shocked at his impulsive request.

"Jeremiah," Beth nearly stuttered, the air from her lungs seeming to be sucked out of her frail body as she quickly tried to compose herself and respond sternly. "I cannot leave my father, this palace, or my people. I have been bound within these stone walls my entire life; it's all I know. I cannot go."

"I'm sorry if I've offended you," Jeremiah softly told her as Beth fully regained her perfect poise, properly standing before Jeremiah.

"Goodnight," Beth clearly told Jeremiah, and then turned away from him, quickly walking to one of the several open doorways to exit the garden area, leaving Jeremiah alone.

After walking across the mossy terrain of the garden, Beth's bare feet then came into contact with the cold stone floor of one of the palace hallways that she had entered in order to exit the garden.

Her head did not turn back once to look at Jeremiah, who had turned away from her himself, and was looking out to the lake one last time before leaving to his room where Elijah was sleeping.

As Beth prepared to turn a corner in the long and straight hallway, she suddenly ran into Royce who was walking in the opposite direction of her, going toward the garden.

"Royce," Beth quickly spoke, startled by his sudden appearance, quickly turning back to see if Jeremiah was coming their way, or if he could see her standing with Royce, but Jeremiah had walked away to a different hallway entrance.

"Beth," Royce quickly responded, placing his hands on her startled shoulders as she took a step away from his chest, which she had practically landed in, "I came looking for you. I see you still spend your nights in the garden."

"Why did you need me?" Beth asked, her thoughts so spun she did not think to remove his hands from her shoulders.

"Beth," Royce spoke to the young princess he had still loved after all these years, "I want you to come with me."

"Where are you going?" Beth asked Royce, unsure of what he meant.

"When I leave for Terrashin tomorrow," Royce explained fully, "I want you to come with me."

"Royce," Beth said, shrugging her shoulders, causing his hands to fall back to his sides, "you know that I can't leave this place. I will not deny my responsibilities here, and become a wanderer as you have."

"Well, it's no longer your decision," Royce told the flustered princess. "By order of my brother, Darius, you will be joining us when we leave tomorrow."

"No!" Beth angrily responded, her own rights to make decisions falling from her hands. "My father would never allow such a thing. He would never have me leave on such a journey unless it was a royal affair, and I were accompanying him."

"The gift we are taking to Terrashin is much greater a deal than you know," Royce told Beth, becoming defensive due to her response to his request. "I can't tell you everything, I just need you to trust me."

"What is he planning?" Beth demanded to know. "What is your brother plotting?"

"Just trust me, Beth," Royce roughly said back. "We will be safe."

"Safe from what?" Beth yelled, slamming her open hands against Royce's chest, causing him to take steps back, away from her. "Tell me what is happening!"

"Beth, calm down!" Royce yelled at Beth, grabbing her wrists tightly, and holding them down at her waist. "I am doing all of this for you. Don't you understand that?"

"For me?" Beth hissed at him, her face turning red with her fury as his hands continued to hold her arms in place, though she had given up on trying to remove them from his grip. "You seem to be the only one getting what he wants. I don't want to go with you, Royce."

"You are coming with me to Terrashin," Royce firmly told her as he loosened his grip from her bound wrists, leaving her arms free where they were in front of her lap. "I just wish you would do so willingly."

"I will warn my father of what Darius is planning," Beth threatened Royce.

"He's gone into solitude until morning," Royce told her. "At sunrise, Darius will be waking him, and staying at his side until he releases us on our journey to Terrashin. There will be no time before then for you to speak with him privately."

"Then I will tell him about the plot right in front of Darius," Beth spoke full of pride in her own strength.

"Beth," Royce continued to argue against her, "What is there to say? You have no evidence, or even an idea of what could potentially be happening. There is nothing to tell your father."

"I will tell him you are aware of it," Beth said back.

"I will deny it," Royce immediately replied.

"You would let your brother have his way?" Beth shockingly asked Royce. "You said you left five years ago because of his plots, and now you defend them?"

"You will be safe, Beth." Royce attempted to reassure her. "We will all be safe."

Beth had no response to give Royce, only her face that was radiating confused emotions as their eyes pierced each other in the dim hallway.

"Will my father be safe?" Beth's shaking voice quietly asked as two tears fell from her reddening eyes, her whole body overtaken with uncertainty and worry.

"I told you," Royce calmly spoke to her, placing his rough thumbs on her soft cheeks, pushing away her tears that were mixed with the black paint circling her eyes, "we will all be safe."

Beth tilted her head down, hiding her face from Royce as his hands moved away from her cheeks.

"We won't be coming back," Beth came to terms with this decision, "will we?"

"The only safe place for us is away from here," Royce confessed as both his and Beth's shoulders sunk downward with the weight of the changes forced upon their lives.

"But my father will be safe?" Beth asked, causing Royce to reach his right hand to the bottom of her chin, and lift her gaze back to his face.

"Yes," Royce reassured her once more, moving his hand from her chin to the side of her thin left arm, "we will all be safe."

"I never thought I would actually leave this place," Beth breathed out, placing her left hand on his extended right arm. "The royal songvis has sung to me about it since I was a child, but I never thought it would actually happen. I thought I would always be bound to this place."

"These stone walls will hold you no more," Royce comforted Beth who was calming down. "And the dangers within it will no longer threaten any of us."

"I still fear for my father in our absence," Beth meekly said.

"You will just have to trust my word," Royce spoke, hoping for a second chance at her trust. "We will all be safe."

"I will trust you," Beth breathed, ending their conversation for the night, both separately departing for their rooms where they were to sleep for the night.

That night, of the four travelers, only Elijah was able to sleep soundly, while the other three toiled over what their futures held. In the morning, the three men travelling stood before King Phillip, Darius, and Beth, on their thrones and stool, prepared to be given full orders.

Because of the momentous occasion that was taking place, many of the capital's most rich and influential men were present, along with the highest level commanders of Terrabeth's military forces. The whole group formed in a half circle around the elevated throne platform, with the three travelers standing at the center, in front of all the other men.

"As you agreed," Darius loudly spoke down to the travelers who had all of their belongings with them, including the sacred belt that was kept in a massive black velvet sack which would hold the other five pieces of armor they were to retrieve, "you will be taking an egg, laid from the royal songvis, and giving it to King Alexander of Terrashin. This offering will be a sign of our permanent peace and alliance with Terrashin. We ask that they raise this soon to be hatched songvis with the greatest of care, and maintain it as a symbol of the love and unity our two Sects will share for one another."

The group of men behind the three travelers all applauded, their clapping hands echoing throughout the throne room, resembling the sound of a thunder calling from the distance, with a violent storm soon to approach. The slaves all stood silently along the walls as they normally did, seeming to be more emotionless than usual.

"And presenting this prize to King Alexander, himself, on our behalf," Darius continued to say, causing the crowd to fall silent again, "will be our dear Princess Beth."

Shocked and happy at the news, Jeremiah clapped along with the men behind him, with Royce jealously taking note of Jeremiah's response. A tall and skinny slave then walked out from behind the platform that held the thrones, and in his hands, lying across his chest, was a faded pink colored egg, practically the height and width of his torso. He walked up to Elijah, and passed it into his arms, with Elijah using all his strength to carry the heavy egg. As this happened, Beth walked from her seat on the stool, down to Elijah, and placed her hand on the seemingly solid egg.

Lights then began to flash from within the egg, revealing a hidden silhouette of the baby songivs inside the egg, the lights coming from the stones across its neck. At this, the crowd again cried out with applause, expecting great things to come to their nation by uniting with Terrashin.

"May Terrabeth forever be the shining light of the Six Sects!" Darius shouted out, causing the applause to increase.

Beth's eyes looked down to Royce's sheathed sword as the realization of Darius' influence woke her to the potential of great destruction in her homeland. Ideas of the danger she was leaving her father in began to haunt her where she stood. She turned her back on the egg to see Darius approaching her as her father safely sat on his throne in a content manner.

Darius' arms extended upward, his face looking to the crowd as they cheered, and Beth took a step toward Royce, placing herself within reach of his sword, leaving her heart to beat at the speed of a star falling in the dead of night.

As Darius stepped down to where the four travelers stood, the world through Beth's eyes began to slow down with every short and quick breath she took. Her thin nostrils flared as her left hand that was in reach of Royce's sword was lightly shaking. In this moment, Beth could end the evil secret agenda of Darius herself, though leaving her guilty of a crime that was punishable by death.

Darius took his final step, now standing on the floor level with the travelers, standing two steps away from Beth. He looked down to see Beth's frightened hand shaking, slowly nearing toward Royce's sword.

"What a brave princess we have!" Darius yelled, snatching Beth's quivering hand, her face becoming shocked as he lifted her hand, spinning her around to face the crowd again, her heart nearly exploding out of her chest. "Who would dare say any other Sect has had a princess willing to travel the world to represent her people so well?"

Beth's eyes blinked rapidly as she tried to calm herself down and appear formal before the applauding crowd, though she could barely keep her mind on a single thought. Darius then lowered her hand, and the crowd became quiet as Beth pulled her hand away from his.

"Along with that compliment, there is a final announcement I have to deliver," Darius proudly spoke out to all those bearing witness in the throne room. "After speaking with our wise and powerful king, he has given me permission to take Princess Beth as my wife."

Again, as though trained to do so, the audience applauded, joyously celebrating the news of the future wedding that would be held in this room where they now stood. Jeremiah, shocked and confused, looked at Beth who, herself, was biting her tongue within her mouth, foaming over with rage at the news as her cheeks began to turn a bloody red shade of hate. Royce, his face expressionless, looked to his brother's sharp face that was graciously accepting the cheers of his followers. Royce then looked to his left side to see his other brother, Derrick, at the end of the arch of gathered men, his arms folded across his chest, grinning wickedly back to Royce.

"Upon her return to Terrabeth, we will be wed!" Darius triumphantly yelled amongst the cheering that only intensified with his additional words.

As the cheering continued, Darius walked up closer to the three traveling men who hesitantly watched his moves.

"You three are to guard Beth and this egg with your lives," Darius told Elijah, Jeremiah, and Royce. "Deliver them both to King Alexander, and once you have done so, you will return my bride to me. Whether you two foreigners return with her here does not affect me, but, you must go with her there."

Darius leaned in toward Elijah, looking him in the eye.

"It's the only way I know my foolish brother will stay on course," Darius whispered. "Were I to leave him alone with this task, the egg would never reach Terrashin, and I would certainly never see him or my bride, again."

Elijah bravely stared back at Darius, not saying a word.

Beth then ran up the platform steps, to her father, falling at his feet, placing her hands into his open palms that were resting on his lap.

"My daughter," King Phillip blindly comforted Beth, gently holding the side of her face with one of his hands, "your journey will only take a few weeks to reach Terrashin's capital city, and then a few more to return. I'm sure your passage will be safe and that I will see you again soon enough. When I do, you will make me proud as a beautiful bride to Darius. He will care for you dearly, and be a strong husband that will protect you."

Beth stared at her father, tears tumbling down onto his robes. With one hand, she gripped tightly his hand on his lap, and with her other, gripped his hand on her face. She did not have a single word to say back to him.

"I have no sons of my own to take my throne after me," King Phillip softly spoke to his daughter. "Darius is the only one I can trust to lead after I am to give up the crown."

Suddenly, Beth felt a hand placed on her shoulder, and she turned around to see Darius standing over her, looking down to where she sat in fear. His sharp facial features were casting shadows across his face, exaggerating his nose and cheekbones.

"You must be off now, my bride," Darius told her as her eyes blazed in fury up to his face. "I dread you leaving, but I am eager for it, so that you will return to me all the sooner."

Beth turned back to her father, and without a word, left a kiss on his right cheek. Her broken eyes looked back to him as he looked at her lovingly, completely blind to what was really upsetting her.

"My beautiful daughter," he said smiling to her, wiping away the one last tear that fell from her, "may you have safe travels."

With that, Beth pulled herself away from her father, and joined the other three travelers that were waiting for her. The four then boarded onto Derrick's ship which was still under the bridge where they had docked weeks ago, and set sail down the Royal River, with Derrick as their captain. He caused no trouble to the four travelers, not even saying a word to any of them as they returned to coast, where Royce's ship and songvissen had been waiting. Beth as well, out of distress from all that was happening, shut herself away, not being seen once by the others on the ship until they reached the market place on the shore, and left Derrick's ship.

They then boarded Royce's ship, still caught up in discord from their time in Terrabeth, and set sail, northwestward, heading for the next continent on their quest: Terrashin.

To be continued in…

Kingdom of Abel
– Song of the Silent –

AUTHOR: Gume Laurel III

Gume graduated from Weslaco East High School in 2005, and afterwards attended a local college. In 2007, he left Weslaco to further his education in Biblical Study. After living in various states in the USA, Gume is currently settled in Milwaukee, WI, where he teaches at Ministers Training Institute, and writes on the side.

His goal in writing the *Kingdom of Abel* series is to share an idea of hope, especially to those who may be in their darkest hour. By assembling this team of Rio Grande Valley natives to produce this series, Gume aims to show people back home that no matter where they come from, they have the opportunity to fulfill their dreams, and can accomplish great things if they determine to.

"There's a path we all must take, from time to time,
in our pursuit of finding purpose.
It is a way filled with loneliness and doubt,
winding through a valley of brokenness,
but with every step taken
there should be a sense of peace and fulfillment,
because it is here that we are most molded
into a person fit to walk into the fullness of our destiny.
So, my friend,
if you desire to reach the fullness of your potential,
embrace this path
... and 'let faith guide your steps, and hope guard your heart.'"

- *Gume Laurel III*

To contact Gume, email him at: gume@kingdomofabel.com

ARTIST: Fabian Puente

Fabian graduated from Weslaco East High School in 2005, and then sought a higher level of education at a local college. In 2006, he moved to Austin, TX to pursue his passion: Art. Since then, he has had his artwork shown in various galleries, and has sold his work at exhibits. Currently, Fabian works for Planet Texas Studios as a 2D Animator, and on the side has his own business called Mom & Pop Studios.

"Through my Art, I hope to inspire others to practice being creative in some way. Artists before me inspired me to pursue this interest, and I hope to accomplish the same thing."

- *Fabian Puente*

To contact Fabian, email him at: mompopstudios@gmail.com
*Photo created by "Crimson Sails Photography"

EDITOR: Celika Casanova

While Celika was born in San Antonio, TX, she was raised in Weslaco, TX, where she graduated from Weslaco High School in 2005. In 2009, she graduated from the University of Texas at Austin with a Bachelors of Science in Human Development and Family Sciences with a concentration in Early Childhood Development. Currently, Celika is back in Weslaco, working at her high school alma mater as a freshman English teacher.

"There's a certain feeling of accomplishment when I see a student has grasped a new idea. Seeing that light go off in their heads, and pride in their eyes, when they learn something new is like no other feeling in the world. As an educator, I hope to see that look in the eyes of my students for as long as I'm blessed to be a teacher. If I have one student come to me in ten years to thank me for teaching them, not only about English and Literature, but what it is to be a successful member of society, everything I am working toward today will be worth every parent-teacher conference, staff development, and headache I've had thus far."

- *Celika Casanova*

To 'Join the Journey,' go to…

Twitter
@Kingdom_of_Abel

Facebook
Facebook.com/KingdomOfAbel

Instagram
@Kingdom_of_Abel

Youtube
Youtube.com/KingdomOfAbel

Website
www.KingdomOfAbel.com

#JoinTheJourney

CPSIA information can be obtained at www.ICGtesting.com
Printed in the USA
LVOW01s0926080414

380797LV00002B/231/P